STA... LEGACY

To Georgia
myths come
True

T. L. Smith

This book is a work of fiction. All characters, places, organizations and events are either the product of the author's imagination or are used fictitiously. Any resemblances are entirely coincidental.

Star People Legacy

Cover Design by T. L. Smith
Cover Art contributing photographers:
Alexeys/iStock by Getty Images
Chesterf/iStock by Getty Images
NASA/CXC/JPL-Caltech/STScI

ISBN-13: 978-1508725077

ISBN-10: 1508725071

ACKNOWLEDGMENTS

Life sends us down many paths and hopefully there are people there to guide and support our journey.

I give a huge thanks to my mother, Patsy, who never discouraged me from doing what I wanted, even if secretly she thought I was crazy for wanting to be a writer.

A hug to the rest of my family for cheering me on from the sidelines: Denita, Adam, Devion, Jayden and Kullen. Alan Stevens, my step-brother, who crossed the country to help out while I was laid up and trying desperately to finish this book. My brother Bill, who introduced me to Science Fiction and let me raid his library. Rick and Brenda Rodriguez, for being my friends when I needed to clear my head, define characters, or just goof off.

A special thanks to Gini Koch, my BFF and a fabulous author, who is always supportive and blunt with her critiques. Every writer needs someone to tell them the truth.

My critique and Beta readers for doing the same, Heather Palmer, Sandra Bowen and Brenda Rodriguez.

The Wyked Women Who Write, who make Cons and book-signings a blast, and collaborate over booze and cupcakes.

And always, I thank the readers who share in my insanity.

Read on!

CHAPTER

1

"Slow down!" I shouted in my helmet mike. "I'm not scrapping you up if you roll."

Sgt. Lutz heard me, slowing a bit and correcting his assent up the ravine. I tapped at the other link on my helmet mike, hooking up to HQ. "Capt. Castle checking in. Ascending to S5-RS3."

"Confirmed Capt. Castle." The voice was a member of Alpha team. They'd head out tomorrow to check Sector Six. "Coming in tonight, Captain?"

"That's the plan. Might even make it before dark."

"I'll let the desk know. Be careful, Beth."

"Always." I tapped out and followed Lutz up the mountain trail. He was the one I had to keep an eye on. He'd been assigned my range partner four months ago and was still new at this.

Most guys thought 4-wheeling was some natural-born talent they were supposed to automatically possess, and didn't like being shown up by a girl.

In the first week Lutz rolled his bike, into a cactus, and had to be airlifted back to the base. Hundreds of cactus spines later, and a lot of ribbing from the team, he learned respect for the bikes, terrain and my warnings.

Unlike Lutz, I'd grown up on wheels, with four brothers in the desert south of Tucson. Told to watch over me, they only heard the words 'watch me' and willingly let me learn the hard way. Within limits. They knew they'd get walloped by our dad if I got seriously hurt. I earned a lot of bruises and abrasions, until I figured out how to handle myself.

So getting assigned to the Border Alliance Team was great. My duty hours were spent 4-wheeling and camping the western Tinajas Mountains of the Goldwater Bombing range, right down to the Mexican border. Easy duty after a stint in the middle-east.

I saw Lutz' right rear wheel spinning out. "Go left. You're in alluvial gravel." I ducked behind my windshield as rocks came flying at me.

"Got ya, Cap." He shifted to the other side of the path. *Yeah, you did.* I rolled up after him. We reached heavier rock, making our accent easier.

As part of the 2050 U.N. Border Alliance Act, relief stations were set up in some of the most geographically dangerous sections of desert. The top of accessible mountains had been leveled off and flagged. On top of these points were lean-to structures and storage boxes. All of this to assist illegal immigration.

Despite continuing political and economic changes in their own countries, immigrants still braved harsh deserts and thieving, murderous Coyotes, just to cross into the United States. Official records listed the Gran Desierto and the Tinajas Mountains as having lower death rates for illegals, but you can't count for what you can't find. These mountains could hide what it killed.

The U.S. Marines maintained the Tinajas and the western border territory on the Goldwater Range. The U.S. Air Force covered the eastern half of the range. The U.S. Army manned several military stretches of the Texas border. The U.S. Border Patrol, restructured in 2022 into a military force, covered all other border lands.

While some political groups objected vehemently to providing aide, I agreed with the policy. Body retrieval was the worst job ever, especially when it involved children. So we gave them food, water and a prayer to survive, so they could be captured later, alive.

Cresting the mountain top, I pulled up next to the radio tower. A large Red Cross banner spun with the winds, a visual invitation for anyone needing assistance. Lutz was already off his 4W and looking around the lean-to. "This is getting weird. We've got nothing."

"Yeah, but we see this. The dead heat of summer changes the migration patterns." I fluttered the collar of my uniform. "They're not stupid." The lightweight fabric wicked off the sweat, but it was still hot as hell out here. "Check the boxes anyway."

I pulled out my range scanner, taking a panoramic picture of the area around the mountain. It would identify any movement in the shrubs, where illegals might be trying to get out of the hot sun and wait until the cooler evening hours to move again. "Nothing."

"Boxes are full, just like the other ones. I get avoiding the summers here, but nothing in over two weeks, at any of the stations along this route."

"Yeah, it is a bit strange." I gave the area a second sweep, considering scenarios. "We prefer they keep to the usual routes and off the bombing ranges." Second worst thing than dead illegals was dead illegals that got bombed because a pilot couldn't see them going a million miles an hour. "I'll check with Delgado when we get back, see if he knows what's up. Maybe the Mexican Army has stepped up patrols on their side."

"Yeah, like that would ever happen." Lutz let the storage lid drop, giving the hasp a crank to keep animals from getting into the box. He picked up the handset on the emergency call box. "Sgt. Brandon Lutz reporting. Sector 5, RS3, negative restock." He hung up when he got a confirmation the call box was working. He grinned as he came back to his 4W. "When do I get to meet this Delgado? We're range partners, virtually siblings, but I still don't know how a Marine ended up with Border Patrol?"

I holstered the scanner. "Sergeant, picking needles out of your ass doesn't make you my brother and it ain't nobody's business who I date." I jerked my head down the mountain. "We got two more boxes to check before we head back."

Lutz snickered. It wasn't the first time he'd razzed me about Delgado, and it wouldn't be the last. He fired up his 4W and took the lead again. I liked to be able to see how he handled the bike. He was infinitely better than when he'd started, but we were heading into rougher terrain. I kept enough distance to see anything dangerous and give him a heads up.

He reached the bottom of the ravine, a natural wash. It wasn't monsoon season yet and there wasn't a cloud in the sky, so I had no worries about flash floods. Driving through the wash was easier than the rocky slopes. He spun his tires in loose sand, but I could tell it was for fun.

I did the same thing as I hit the wash, then continued to follow him. We'd go up the wash a few miles to the next relief station. Most of the boxes were near washes. They provided easier footing for the illegals, water if it was the rainy season, and the flags identifying the drop boxes were easy to see. Driving along them was easier too. My mind went to Delgado.

Lutz was right about our unusual relationship. There was no animosity between the Marines and Border Patrol, any more than there was between us and any other branch of the services. But there wasn't much of a future either. The military transferred us regularly. I managed to extend this assignment, because of my unique qualifications, but that privilege had its limit. For the first time in any relationship, I didn't know what to do.

I hit a dip, bouncing hard. *Damn!* This was not the time or place to figure it out. I shoved my personal problems down again.

The next relief station was coming up. Lutz slowed down, looking for the trail. This deep into the mountains the only paths were created by wild animals, illegals or us. I checked out the sandy wash for footprints. Nothing.

Reaching the summit took a lot longer this time. Coming from the Mexico side was easier, but the U.S. face of this particular section of the range had a lot of steep drop offs. It took us a good hour to reach the top.

I did the scans while Lutz checked the site. He slammed the lid on the storage box. "Not a single bottle of water missing. I might be new, but I can smell wrong and this totally reeks."

"I agree, but let me check out a few things before raising any alarms." Lutz scowled at me as he got back on his 4W. I ignored him, calling HQ. "This is Capt. Castle. Moving on to final check point."

"Confirmed Team Bravo."

"Come on Sargent, one more checkpoint. Then back to base and a cold beer."

He looked out at the final hilltop, the flag visible from this point, as were the other three. "I tell you, I got a sick feeling about this." He continued to scowl. "Last thing I want is to find a ditch of bodies."

CHAPTER

2

Relief Station Five was the most dangerous. It was the closest to the Mexican border. Sometimes we got shot at from across the fence. Bad shots, or they were only trying to scare us. Border Patrol often reported the same attacks, and a few with fatal results.

We returned to the dried up mountain wash, but this time I took the lead. As we reached a fork in the wash, I noticed something odd. Stopping my 4W, I waved Lutz to join me.

I also grabbed a stick, whacking the rocks as I edged along the side of the wash. “Go away, my little friends.” As a kid I learned to warn rattlesnakes of my presence. They much more preferred to leave of their own accord, than be stepped on or otherwise surprised.

Lutz followed me a few yards into the other wash. “What’s up?”

I knelt down, looking at the ground. “See the patterns in the sand?” I mimicked them with my hand. “Someone was through here and attempted to hide it.”

He knelt down, looking at the swishes. “I see what you’re pointing at, but I don’t get it.”

I shook my head. “People get this idea that if you rake out the sand behind you, you can hide your footprints, but I can see the swiping movements. The patterns aren’t natural.”

Seeing a loose branch of Palo Verde, I broke off the limb. “Walk out and back.”

Lutz did what I asked. Then I did the swishing, wiping out his footsteps. “That’s what you have left.”

“Ohhhh-kay, I see it.” He shifted to look up the wash. “Someone did the same thing.”

“Yeah.” I walked out to where I’d started the swishes. “If you want to do it right, you have to alternate swishes with whacks.” I randomly beat the tracks to show him what I meant. “Now it looks more like tumbleweed rolled through here, than some deliberate attempt to hide footsteps.”

“Intel teach you all this?

“No, playing hide-n-seek with my brothers.” I tossed the stick away.

“Wow, Cap, you had one strange childhood.” He laughed as he examined my handiwork.

You wouldn’t believe it. I headed back for my 4W. “Let’s see how far this goes.”

He followed me. “I assume the swishes told you they went up the wash, not down it?”

"Angles and depths." I eased my vehicle along the wash's edge, keeping my eyes on the sand marks. The further we went, the more consistency I saw in the marks. My back started to itch and a shiver crept over me. "Okay, sergeant. Something definitely does stink."

I rolled to a stop and got off my 4W, sticking close to the wash edge where Terote trees provided some cover. "Hold, while I get a scan of this." I got at an angle where the light showed the grooves in the sand. I followed a track long enough to show the predictable repeats in the patterns. "This is artificial."

"I thought we already established that." Lutz's voice sputtered in my headphones.

"You're cracking up. Check your frequency."

"I'm getting static from you too."

Tapping at the controls on my helmet I could see our channel wasn't running at peak. I tried retuning it, but only got more noise, until I started walking back in his direction. "Hmmm, something's interfering on this frequency."

"Clearer now. What about base?"

"HQ, this is Team Bravo. Do you read me? HQ… this is Bravo…" I waited for even a burst of static indicating they heard me, but the airwaves were dead. *Shit! This isn't right at all.* "There's no reason to be unable to reach the base, let alone each other when we were only a few meters apart."

Lutz was up on his foot rests, looking through binoculars. "There's a tower right there. We should be hearing something."

Being out of com range was bad enough. Being out of range when something was wonky... "We need to get out of here."

The words barely left my mouth before there was the scrunching of gravel up the wash. From around the bend came a Hummer SUV painted in desert camo. They threw up gravel and dust as they skid to a stop. Seeing them gave me a moment of relief. Someone was running an exercise out here and HQ didn't think to tell us.

Just then two more Hummers rolled up behind us, blocking us in. As they got out of their vehicles, relief was sucked out of me. Lutz was almost as fast as I was at drawing our weapons, covering my back as I faced the first group of men. Also armed and guns pointed at us.

"This is the Yuma Proving Grounds. Unless you can provide proper documentation, you are trespassing on government property, a federal offense." Judging from positions and posture, I picked out the leader of this group and planted the bead of my weapon's targeting system in the middle of his forehead. "You've got ten seconds to drop your weapons and identify yourselves. Eight, seven, six…"

Shoot, shoot now! That thought and the counting were competing with each other. Eight men in non-military camo fatigues outgunned us, but we couldn't show any weakness. We were Marines and this was our turf. "Five..." I had a bead on the man and the marksmen pins proved I could put him down in one shot, and his driver, before his people started shooting.

The man didn't take his eyes off me, but put his hand on his driver's gun, pulling it down as he took a step closer to me. "Capt. Castle. No need for threats."

What the fuck? I almost said it out loud, but held steady. "Knowing my name doesn't impress me. Three seconds."

He held one hand out, reaching to the shirt pocket. "I've got my credentials right here."

I held my fire as he approached. "Stop right there. Put them on that rock and back off." I kept my bead on him. He complied, dropping folded pages on a large boulder.

He backed away as I made my way to the rock. "We're here legally, running security for a research program."

"And that makes you think you can draw weapons on us?" I shook out the papers. I'd worked with enough civilian contractors to know they looked real. Military. A company's name at the top, a general's signature, located at the pentagon, DOD certification, nature of business… Top Secret. *As if the red letters boldly slashed across the pages didn't already tell me that.*

"As you can see, my papers are in order, so you can lower your weapons."

"You first." I tossed the papers back, not carrying that they hit the ground. "You're the guests and you pulled guns in our house."

He cocked his head at me, giving me a slight smile that wasn't friendly in the least. "For the last mile you've left base territory and are on the federal reservation."

"Don't try to pull that crap on me. The entire mountain range falls under our jurisdiction. Our fucking house, so holster your weapons or I call for backup."

"Go ahead." He continued that smile.

He knew I had no com.

After a few more seconds he let the smile shift, not faking the friendly anymore. "Get back on your RVs and roll out of here. No harm, no foul."

This wasn't a situation where I could stand my ground. "Sgt. Lutz. Mount up."

He hesitated, but did as I ordered. I kept my gun on this gang's leader. That smirk was back on his face as he nodded. "Good choice. And I suggest you keep this encounter to yourselves. I'm sure, Capt. Castle, you know the penalty for blowing a Top Secret operation."

"You file your reports and I'll file mine." I backed towards my 4W.

He followed after me. "No reports. I'm trying to be nice just letting you go. You file a report and by dinnertime you'll be in handcuffs. My bosses will bury you and anyone you tell in a hole until our mission is over, and likely forget you're there."

"Threats? Really?" I swung my leg over the saddle, without dropping the bead on his forehead. "You just keep being the inhospitable guest."

He leaned over the front of my 4W, nearly putting his head to my gun. "Keep your mouths shut and your asses on the other side of the line and you'll never know we're here."

His eyes were small beady black dots as he glared at me, but this close, something else struck me. A flash of another being, floating around, through him, like a ghost. My heart started beating harder. Despite my upbringing, I didn't believe in Spirits. Until now. Something unnatural was attached to this man and it was evil. Every nerve in my body wanted to twitch, but I held onto my training.

Show no fear. "Back off. My finger is starting to get a mind of its own and it doesn't like you any better than I do."

He smirked as he turned away and walked back towards his vehicle.

CHAPTER 3

The armed men let us drive between them, but never took their weapons off us. I looked at the Hummers. They were the real models, made for this exacting terrain. The rear windows were tinted black, making it impossible to see inside. I got the impression there were people inside. I also got a wave of something else, like a smell of desperation.

Guns waved us on. At the rear of each vehicle were drag plates. That explained the consistent patterns in the sand. Even as we cleared their blockade, there were no tire tracks behind them. As we hit a curve I threw the Smirker one last look. He glared back at me. Even at a distance, he tried to intimidate me. With that evil Spirit around him, it worked. I held my breath until we were clear of these intruders.

Lutz dropped back to ride beside me, raising his visor. "We need to report this."

"I'll deal with it." I studied the terrain around us, looking for the traps we'd sprung to tell these people we were even here. "First, let's clear the last relief station and get back to base."

He gave me a look that said he thought I was nuts, but he didn't question my order. As soon as we reached the main wash, the static on my com line cleared. HQ was calling me, sounding pretty persistent and annoyed.

"This is Capt. Castle."

"What happened? You should have checked in from RS5 by now."

"Sorry, we were investigating tracks. Only realized a few minutes ago that our coms were down. On our way to RS5 now." Lutz cleared his throat, but I shook my head. "Will reach the relief station in another ten minutes."

Having set a deadline, I took the lead again, picking up our pace. It also kept Lutz from asking me a bunch of questions. With the interference the conversation with these intruders hadn't transmitted, but I'd recorded the Smirker and his papers. I wanted to go over the information before I did anything official.

The last relief station was close enough to the border we could almost throw a rock and hit Mexico. It was also the first point of relief for illegals, and the heaviest hit. By the time they reached this point they were out of food and water.

Lutz confirmed what we already knew, that the boxes were undisturbed. We reported in, informing them we were headed back to base. I kept radio silence as we passed the branch of the washes. All evidence we'd been up that way had been erased. I didn't say anything to Lutz.

We maintained radio silence until we broke out of the mountains. Then I pulled over, removed my helmet, and walked back along the path a few meters. Lutz was right there, helmet off too. "So why the silent treatment?"

"They were listening to us."

"Our coms weren't working."

"Theirs were. He called me by name and when I threatened to call for backup, he dared me to do it." I stared into the darkening mountains. "I had my mike full open and HQ didn't pick up on any of it."

"Why didn't they warn us anyone was up there?" Lutz fidgeted as he looked back into the hills too. "That almost came down to a shootout."

"Which we'd have lost." I turned back towards our 4Ws.

"Is that what you're reporting?" Lutz followed.

"I'm not sure what I'm reporting. Not until I get more information." I hesitated putting my helmet on again, not trusting it now. "I'm not one to jump at conspiracy theories, but I got a bad feeling about this, like you got a bad feeling about the illegals."

"Maybe they're related."

You think? I didn't need to be snippy with Lutz. "Wouldn't be surprised. If that's how they treated us, no telling what they'd do to anyone else. But before I go blowing any whistles I need to know if they're legit. Making noise could be career-enders for both of us."

Lutz's new scowl was understandable. He'd just reenlisted. We'd chatted enough to know getting thrown out of the Marines was not acceptable. "Yeah, let's cover our asses first."

Reluctantly I put on my helmet, confirmed we were heading to our camp. We loaded the 4Ws into our truck and I let Lutz drive. It was a long, wordless ride back to base. We checked our vehicles into maintenance, our helmets into the com office and grabbed our duffels. I had two days to turn in a formal report, so I hung onto our data chips. Outside HQ doors I dismissed Lutz, returning his salute and went in by myself.

I half-expected the duty officer to be waiting, to admonish me for the break in communications. Another part of me expected our CO to debrief me for violating a secure area. But the duty officer barely looked up from his desk. "Relief stations checked out? Vehicles and gear checked in?"

"Everything should be restocked and ready to head out tomorrow." I ran my arm over the ID scanner, electronically signing the mission log. "Anything before I call it a night?"

He shrugged. "No messages in the system. Ready to cool off with a cold one?"

"As soon as I wash off the dust." I wanted to leave, but I kept waiting for some huge boot to drop on my neck.

He noticed my lingering, actually looking up at me over the top of his smart glasses. "Is there something else you need, Captain?"

"No, no…" I faked a laugh, pulling my hat from my waistband. "On my way out."

No one stopped me as I headed back through the building and out into the evening heat. Or as I plodded through the parking lot to my car. With a tap of my key fob my car chirped and started up, the air conditioner preset at full. I held the door open for a moment to let hot air out, but also one last verification someone wasn't going to drag me off to a dark room for a ten-hour interrogation.

No one lurked in the dusky shadows. I started to get into my car, but dropped my keys. Bending down, I saw marks on the asphalt, scuffs that ran up under my car. It had been days since I parked. Dust storms had deposited several layers of sand on and around my car, so there was no doubt something had recently been next to my car, pushed up under it.

Shit, shit, shit! I cursed in my head as I picked up my keys. I'd pulled embassy duty in the Middle-East for my first military posting. Cars were a favorite target of attack. A million procedures ran through my head in that few seconds. It wasn't attached to my ignition. It might be pressure sensitive, waiting for me to sit down, or attached to the drive shaft, waiting for the vehicle to move. Or I was being watched and it was radio controlled.

Did that mean they were possibly listening too? Maybe it was just a tracking device. If I was being monitored, standing here was certainly going to raise questions. *Say something. Look like you forgot something.* I took a few steps away from my car, letting the door auto-close. "Why do I always forget?" I pretended to wander back towards HQ, pulling out my phone.

I got Delgado's inbox. "Hey, babe. I forgot to charge up again. Can you come and get me? I'll meet you at the club."

CHAPTER

4

The base tram was near the corner so I ran the last few meters. It was packed and noisy. I pocketed my phone and looked around. A buzz-topped E-1 stood behind me. "Private, my phone's dead, can I borrow yours?"

He stared at me for a moment, his mouth opened slightly. He looked fresh out of boot camp. "Yes… Yes, ma'am!" He dug in his pocket and produced a phone.

"Thanks." I dialed Lutz. "Been out on the range all week and forgot." I turned my back on him and relied on the noise to drown me out. Lutz answered. "Dude. The club. Now!"

"What…"

"NOW!" I hung up, no explanation and quickly dialed another number.

"Hello, Officer Delgado here." I knew he'd pick up this number, no matter what. It was his emergency number for disasters.

"Casey." My heart skipped a beat to hear his voice.

"Where you calling me from and why do you need me to pick you up? I charged your car before you went on duty."

"I know. Something happened. Can't explain right now. Come get me."

"I'll be there in… thirty minutes."

I disconnected and turned back to the private. "Thank you, again."

"No problem, ma'am." He bowed his head, saluting not required here.

I focused on the ride. If they were watching, or listening, I'd need to remain somewhere noisy. The tram and the bar both qualified. It took nearly a half-hour to reach the club, where most the riders got off. I was able to stay wedged between the kid and some old Master Sergeant, until we slipped out of the broiling heat and into the cool dark club.

The guys were gentlemen and let me up to the bar first, where I grabbed a can of beer. Not seeing Lutz or Casey, I headed on through the building to the gym on the back side, with a locker room. I had looked forward to getting home and hitting the pool for a nighttime swim. Instead I had to settle for a quick shower.

I shivered through a cold shower, getting the grim off and giving me a surge of energy. I kept a vacuum-sealed bag in my duffle, a set of civvies for emergencies. Levis, a clean sports bra and a tank top. I let my hair out of the tight knot I kept hidden by my cap. A good spray of dry shampoo and a brushing fluffed it out and made it smell decent again.

With a glance in the mirror and I was not the captain in desert brown BDUs, but a petite, dark-skinned local hanging at the club. Plenty of the young Cocopah girls worked on base and while I wasn't one of the River People, white people didn't know the difference.

Not the same rule among the Native Americans. On paper I was Navajo, but there was an unspoken family secret about our true heritage. My parents didn't speak of it except in veiled comments, promising I'd learn the truth 'when the time was right'.

At nearly 29 years old, I wasn't holding my breath for that truth. I'd graduated high school with scholarships and got accepted into the U.S. Military Academy for the Marine Corps. I came out with honors, lieutenant bars and a degree in linguistics. No surprise there. I spoke Navajo on the Res, Spanish on the back streets of Tucson, and English for the white schools. I picked up French and Arabic at the academy, easily adding two more regional dialects during my first tour of the Middle East.

Picked up two more middle-east languages on my second tour. Along with a bullet wound, temporary hearing loss in one ear and a tattoo I didn't hide, or flash around either. If you were a Marine, you knew what it meant. With all that, I still hadn't achieved that mystical point where my true heritage could be revealed.

I stared at myself in the mirror. *Why do you suddenly care? Today?*

"Because you're 29." I answered myself out loud. "I'm old enough to know the truth."

I leaned closer to the mirror. I didn't look 29, even after all these years in deserts from here to the middle-east. My raven black hair hung down past my shoulder blades. Sun had baked my cheekbones, making me a bit darker and the sharper angles of my face a bit more pronounced. But in a good way. I needed virtually no makeup. Maybe a little mascara for a night out. I was 'sun-kissed'. That's what Casey called it.

Except for the tattoo, I didn't look like a Marine. I still wore the same Levis as I did in high school, patching them up whenever needed with some bohemian embroidery I learned as a little kid. The Levies fit a lot better now than they did when I was 17, all velvety soft.

The fitted tank top showed off defined arm muscles and shoulders, without looking like I was trying out for some bodybuilder's magazine. And I had a good cleavage, no implants or pushup bras needed. I didn't go for the 'girly' stuff, but didn't mind proving I wasn't a 'man with boobs', as some idiots assumed when they heard about a female Marine.

Some people joked that if I was a foot taller, I could be a supermodel, but I was happy at five-four. Not too intimidating, unless I needed to be. Being petite worked out fine interrogating a suspect. They always went for what they believed was my weakness, leaving them almost defenseless when I came back on them. Play to your strengths. A well-learned lesson.

Right now I didn't want to be intimidating. I wanted to blend in so I could get out of here incognito. *You're just one of the girls.* I fluffed my hair again. Casey and Lutz were probably waiting for me. I checked my weapons, zipped up my duffel and stashed it in the locker, making sure it was secured.

Heading back into the bar, I ran into a cluster of the 'girls'. In uniform I was 'La Capitana'. Out of uniform I was one of the gang, except I wasn't looking to marry a military man. Since I wasn't competition, they elevated me to girlfriend status.

After some girly screams and hugs, we leaned against the bar to scope out the evening's choices. I was good at screening out the married men and one-nighters, and preached to the younger girls to stay away from the newbies fresh out of boot camp. Those boys were far from home, family and friends. It wasn't a surprise when they latched onto the first set of boobs pointing their direction. They were easily led down the aisle and it seldom ended well.

Delgado didn't like me giving man-hunter tips, but I'd rather be a matchmaker than see the fallout of a short marriage, eighteen years of child support and a lifetime of resentment. That the girls listened to me meant they wanted more too.

I pointed out the young man from the tram, putting the nix on him. Scanning the room for better catches, I saw Delgado watching me from a corner table. *Thank you, God!* Surprisingly, Lutz sat across from him, both leaning their chairs up against the wall. I didn't have to ask how they met up. Casey, Officer Ricardo Castro Delgado, was still in uniform and wore it so well it got my heart beating for a whole different reason. "You're on your own, girls."

"Ohhh, your man's here." One of the girls snickered over my shoulder. "And your yummy friend too. Together?" She gave me a raised eyebrow.

"He's my patrol partner. Don't make anything of it." I left them, weaving my way through the tables.

Both men dropped their chairs and got up as I approached. “Beth.” Casey gave me a kiss. Quick and simple. Neither of us were much on PDA.

“Glad to see introductions are done.” The two men looked at each other and shrugged. Good, no macho posturing, though Casey’s arm was around me, his hand stroking my back.

Despite our usual avoidance of being touchy-feely, I wanted his arms around me. Deep down in my guts I knew I was in some kind of trouble I wasn’t prepared for. For the first time ever, I wanted him to protect me, but I couldn’t give in to irrational fear. I needed a clear head. I pointed to Lutz’s phone pocket, wiggling my fingers. “Were you already here?”

“I was on my way.” He frowned, taking his phone out and handing it to me.

I took my own out. There was an ancient large stereo speaker behind our table, the jukebox was already cranking out old 70-80’s music. I put the phones on top the speaker. Delgado volunteered his own. He leaned over my shoulder, but looked at Lutz as he whispered. “What the hell is up?”

CHAPTER

5

He listened as I quickly described what happened in the mountains, only stopping as a fresh round of beers appeared. I told him about the undisturbed drop boxes and the strange men who cornered us, threatened us. That they had been monitoring us enough to know our names. Then the marks under my car.

I left out the weird images that surrounded the Smirker. I wasn't so sure they were real. Maybe too much heat. If not for Lutz having the same experience, I might have written the entire day off to hallucinations.

Casey looked worried. "I haven't been getting reports of upped patrols across the border, but we have noticed a drop in numbers too. Our analysts are looking at other parts of the fence to see if we need to reassign assets. It could be that it's just been hotter this summer."

"It hasn't stopped them before." I stared at Lutz. "Four days, eighteen drop boxes. Two separate runs. No hits.

How many grabs have you made of people who came through the Tinajas this month?" Casey's face crinkled, confirming what I thought. *None.* "We both got bad feelings these freaks might have something to do with it."

Lutz backed me up with a nod.

"A group close to the relief stations, and too 'secret' for anyone to give you a heads up that they're around..." Casey still wasn't on board with our suspicions. "Not the first time agencies didn't share info. None of the other patrols reported anything strange?"

"They're not as good as me. I wouldn't have noticed, except for the mistakes they made covering their tracks. You can bet your sweet ass everyone else definitely missed the signs."

Lutz gave an eye roll and opened his mouth, but Casey held his hand up to stop him. "She's not boasting. I've been out hunting with her and she never comes home empty-handed. Ever." Casey let out a sigh. "Okay, so this group stops you, warns you to stay away and to keep your mouths shut, then lets you go. Why would they screw with your car? They had you out where you could disappear and it would take days, weeks, or never to find your bodies."

"I don't know. Because it would bring more people into the mountains looking for us?"

"So they rigged your car. Did they screw with yours?" Casey looked to Lutz.

"Don't have one. Girlfriend's driving it out next month."

"Have you been to your room yet?" I darted my eyes around the bar, feeling that itch between my shoulders again as the topic turned to possible sabotage. "You don't have a roommate and you've been gone for four days."

"No, but barracks room, cars?" Lutz leaned further across the table. "It makes no sense. Attacking us here runs the risk of injuries or deaths. That would put the entire military on alert. Everything we'd done for weeks, months, would be scrutinized looking for motives, including our patrols."

"Maybe it's not a bomb. Maybe it's a tracking device." Casey tossed out the words, the same thought I'd let cross my mind in the parking lot.

"No." I shot the idea down. "They shove trackers into a wheel-well or under a bumper. Whatever it is, I don't want to hop in and find out." I finished my second beer. Drinking wasn't a good idea with this crap going down, but Lutz and I both needed them.

"Then we should go take a look at Lutz' room." Casey slid his chair out, jerking his head at Lutz. "We'll go over and look for tampering. You stay here, in case someone is watching."

"I'm better at looking for that stuff than you are."

"Yeah, but you're the probable target. So stay here." He kissed my cheek, but his hands squeezed my shoulders a bit hard, emphasizing he didn't want to argue with me. Lutz hoisted his duffel over his shoulder, no arguing either.

"Okay. I'll order another round, so make it fast."

I shifted over to Casey's chair, getting my back to the wall and watched them leave the bar. The lighting over this spot was non-existent, creating more shadow. I could look out across the room and be barely noticeable.

When the waitress walked by, I ordered our drinks. At this hour, with this crowd, it would take a while.

Temporary quarters wasn't far, less than a block. They might even be back before the drinks arrived.

They'd check out his door, maybe talk to anyone who was around. Then head back. I wanted them back here. Both of them. Maybe it was better to get Lutz off base for a few days. He wouldn't object. Without a car, he was stuck on base until his girlfriend moved out here.

He was eager to see her again and set up house. She'd already be here except for the waiting list for housing. As his common-law partner, they qualified under the revised 'spousal' regulations.

While I didn't share a lot about my personal life, Lutz did. I already knew everything about Sabrina. She was a civilian nurse and they'd met during his first tour of duty, before he got shipped off to Afghanistan. They maintained a long-distance relationship until he got back and was stationed at Quantico. She moved in with him there to see if it worked.

It did and now she was uprooting her east-coast life to relocate to a desert, lock, stock, pit bull and kitty. The wedding was scheduled for November, when their relatives could come out and not be roasted alive. That was the plan and Lutz constantly lamented their forced separation.

"He's so annoying..." *OMG, I'm jealous.* The thought was a strange one to cross my mind. Was I really jealous? Casey and I were arguing a lot about our relationship. I didn't want to leave the Marines and he didn't want to leave Border Patrol. I'd been here for three years, but the Marines weren't going to leave a linguist sitting stateside. Betting odds put me back in the Middle-East. Our split was inevitable, something he refused to accept.

Yet, since our run in with the freaks in the mountains, all I wanted was Casey. I wanted him here, right now, even though I could take care of myself. I wanted Casey and every nerve in my body wanted me to get up and run down the street to find him. I rubbed my forehead, trying to dislodge the overwhelming urges. That dreaded itch between my shoulders got worse.

The waitress appeared, putting down our drinks, three cans of cold beer, then a half-filled pint of dark beer and a shot of something that looked like Irish Cream. She set both glasses in front of me and started picking up the empties.

"That's not ours. We just want the beer."

"Oh, someone sent it over to you." She smiled at me. "As if you don't already have enough admirers."

"Really? Who sent it and what is it?"

"The guy right over…" She looked back towards the bar. "Dang it, he was there a minute ago. Big guy, brown-blonde hair, older. Wasn't in uniform, so can't tell you more." She looked for another couple seconds and shrugged. "I'm sure he'll show up soon enough." She pointed to the little shot glass. "Drop this in the beer and drink it down fast. It's called an Irish Car Bomb."

"A what?" I reached for my phone, then remembered it was on top the speaker. All three were on the speaker. "I need to see this guy." I stood up, searching the room.

"I'm sorry." She looked around the bar again. "Do you want me to take it back?"

She started to reach for the drink. "No. Leave it."

"Yes, ma'am." She glanced around the bar again, then slinked back through the tables.

I'd only gotten an up-close look of the Smirker. I'd easily recognize him, but no one else in his group. Her description was too vague to know if it was him or not, but I continued to scan the room, sitting down, trying not to look freaked out. "Where are you, asshole?"

"Dina, what's wrong?" Yazzie, the oldest of the local girls threw herself into the chair next to me. "Your Spirit is radiating fear."

I reeled myself back in, not knowing I was letting my alarm show. But no one else was looking at me. Just Yazzie, who the others said was the Cocopah's next tribal spiritualist.

She leaned in close. "Since you arrived, your Spirit has been disturbed. A darkness has crossed over your light. If a bad Spirit has attached itself to you, you must be careful." She reached out and grabbed my hand, slipping something small and hard into my palm. "Keep this with you. Your Spirit is stronger than the evil that pursues you."

"Yazzie, I'm not into all that…"

She waved me silent, closing my hand around the rock. "Keep it with you always so your Spirit touches the Earth. You are not Kwapa, but you are of old blood and your Spirit is stronger. Trust it, Dina, even if you don't understand it."

She slipped away without any more warnings. I reached for my can of beer when it struck me. "Wait!" I shouted, standing to catch Yazzie. But she was gone. That fear wasn't any lighter.

She'd called me Dina.

CHAPTER

6

I sat down and let the rock fall to the table. A clear stone, rough, but polished by hands over a long period of time. A local rock… a quartz? I didn't know. I couldn't think. My head spun with the confusion crashing down on me. I pressed my palms to my temples, squeezing my head between them. *This is all insane! It can't be real.*

"Beth?" I jumped out of my seat at a hand settled on my shoulder. Casey. His pushed me back down as he sat next to me. "Easy, love."

I rubbed my eyes, looking at Casey, then at Lutz standing behind him. "They were here, in the bar."

"Where?" Lutz jerked his head around to glare at the crowd. His hand poised to reach under his shirt.

"Sit down and keep your hand away from your gun or you'll get us all arrested." Casey hissed at Lutz, who obeyed quickly. Casey sat down and stroked my arm. "They approached you here?"

“No. They sent that!” I pointed to the drink. “It’s an Irish Car Bomb.”

“Are you kidding?” He pushed the drink away and his jaw clenched. “That’s taking it too far. We’re going to finish our drinks and get out of here. Lutz is coming with us.”

“So his room was… visited?”

“Yeah, someone was there.” Lutz grabbed his beer and gulped part of it down. “Didn’t find or take anything. I think they’re just trying to scare us.”

“And they’re succeeding.” Casey’s voice was low, but strong. “You’re both worn out and stressed. You’re going to sleep it off and we’ll look at everything again in the light of day.”

“Yeah, let’s do that.”

Casey swung back and grabbed the phones off the speaker, handing them to me.

I pulled the back of mine off and removed the card, giving Lutz his. He pulled his card too. “We’ll pick up burners for any real conversations.”

“Sounds like a beer run.” Casey pocketed his phone. He couldn’t disconnect from his office at all, but we were the only ones he needed to talk to.

Lutz grabbed the Car Bomb. He dropped the shot in and drank the beer down, making a face. “Nah, had better. Should we grab the car?”

Casey looked at the beers. “No. Besides drinking, you’re both too distracted to drive. Drink up and we’ll go.”

We finished our drinks, trying to look casual. I got my duffel from the locker room and met them at the gym door.

I wanted my own gun in reach, shifting my favorite from inside the duffle to the outer pocket, the grip turned for an easy grab.

Lutz crawled into the back seat of Casey's big truck and stretched out. I took shotgun, the duffle between my feet, but leaning over the center console to be closer to Casey. Security waved us out the back gate, taking us the long way through a rougher side of town.

At a little bodega, Casey stopped and bought beer. He handed me a bag. In it were chips and three burner phones. I quietly set them up and passed them out. When we got to our apartment, I went out onto the patio while Casey settled Lutz into the guest bedroom.

We were on the third floor of a five story complex, facing the pool. Feeling movement behind me, I couldn't help but look around a little too fast. Casey stuck his head out the door. "I'll fix dinner. Want a drink?"

I shook my head and he went back inside. I didn't need more beer. I needed to make a call. It only rang twice.

"Din'ah!"

"Yes, mama." Of course she would know it was me, despite the strange number on her caller ID. The tears that had been pushing at the back of my eyeballs started to break free. "Mama, something bad is happening."

"I know my daughter. I can feel Spirits stirring."

"Mama, someone called me by my name. One of the Kwapa."

"A medicine woman."

"She knew I wasn't of the River People, and called me Dina."

"She must be strong among the Earth Spirits. If you are in danger, they told her. What did she say to you?" My mother's voice was filled with concern, but was also demanding.

"She said the same thing… that a dark Spirit passed over me. She gave me a rock…" I dug into my pocket. "She said to keep it with me always."

"Then you must do as she says. River People worship the Earth Spirits. The rock is a talisman to keep these Spirits around you, until you can draw them yourself." There was a pause on her end. "That is not what scares you. What have you seen?"

She always knew if we were hurt or in trouble. "I don't know." I looked back into the apartment. Casey was in the kitchen. "I was on patrol up in the mountains and ran into people who didn't belong there. One of them got close to me and I think I saw something, like a ghost, clinging to him. It wasn't him, but still part of him. It was… evil."

There was an audible shuttering sigh through my phone. "We have hunted these dark Spirits for decades, sure they were hiding from us somewhere near."

"Who are they, who is… us? Is this part of the secret?"

"It is not easy to explain, my child. Your brothers are on their way. Your father is coming to get me, then we will join you too."

"What? Mom, they're all over the country. You can't make them come out here because some strange man scared the shit out of me."

"It is more than that. I felt it begin for you, the Rising, driven by this enemy. We must be there. We must all be there." I could hear her tone changing, as if she was about to go into one of her prayer chants.

"MOM!"

"Din'ah." She wasn't gone yet.

"I need answers. What's so important you have to come here?"

"My honored daughter." She sighed again. "There is much to tell you, but I must be there in person. However, so you can try to understand, do you remember your tribal elements?"

"Of course. Air, Earth, Fire and Water."

"Yes, they compose this world and represent all the peoples, human and animal, residing upon her, but there are two elements not of this world."

I hesitated. "Star and Underworld."

"We are of the Star People. The man you saw is owned by the Maxa'xak, an evil Spirit. Evil Spirits of the Underworld appear often on this world, but none are like this one. Entire tribes have perished at their will, such as the Yahi. We failed the Yahi. We will not fail this time, not if you are Rising."

"Rising, what the heck is that supposed to be?"

"Your Star Spirit has been awakened outside of ritual, which means she is powerful. Seeing this evil Spirit was only possible if she is rising to the surface?"

"She? Rising? Mom, I don't get any of this."

"Are there other conflicts in your life?" Her voice was firmer, demanding.

A rapping on the patio door made me turn around again. Casey held several plates, cans of beer tucked between his arm and body, wanting me to let him out. "Yes, there is, with Casey. With me being a Marine."

"I thought as much. I have seen his Spirit. It is pure. Star people can only be attached to those of pure Spirit."

Casey raised his eyebrows at me when I didn't rush to open the door. "What's that have to do with anything?" I slipped around the table. "I need to know what to do." With a jerk I pulled the glass door open.

"We cannot reveal our names to anyone except pure Spirits. He is pure. Tell him." She sighed as if tired. "Tell him, but do nothing until we arrive."

Before I could protest, she hung up. I pocketed the phone and grabbed two of the plates from Casey. "Where's Lutz?"

"Passed out. I left him a plate in case he wakes up." I got out of his way and he slipped past me to the table. He got everything down without dropping or spilling. "Left over Carne Asada and tortillas."

"And a salad."

"Yeah, well I know what you live on out there. Sit down." I did, my back to the wall where I could see inside and out into the courtyard. He took the chair against the door. "Who were you talking to?"

"My mother." I said it without looking at him, maybe because our conversation had taken such a strange twist to include him. "Had to let her know… had to… "

"Hey, darling…" He grabbed my hand. "…I know how you are with your family. I figured you'd call her. Let's eat and then you need to sleep."

I could only nod in agreement. Everything my mother said was slamming around in my head, enough it was starting to hurt. Everything she didn't tell me was making my imagination spin. And she wanted me to tell him the truth about myself.

I wasn't sure if I could.

CHAPTER

7

Food made a difference, relieving some of the headache, giving me some energy, enough to make it into the bath Casey started for me. Not a skimpy bath, like my old apartment. Our incomes afforded us a luxury apartment, three bedrooms, two baths, with all the amenities we could want, including a spa tub

I climbed into the pile of bubbles the air jets created. The water was hot as I sank deeper into the vibrating pulses. Tight aching muscles instantly started to relax.

Casey gave me a good fifteen minutes before joining me. I leaned back as his arms wrapped around me. “Better?”

“Now.”

“Hmmm…”

There was a tone to his voice, but he wouldn't say anything until I did. And he expected me to. It worked. "What?"

"That's pretty much the only word you've said since your phone call."

"No it's not." I could feel the rumble in his chest starting, another monosyllable humph. "Okay, I have a lot on my mind."

"No doubt, but more so after talking to your mother. You know you can trust me."

"Infinitely." I closed my eyes and laid my head back against his shoulder. "More than anyone I ever met, besides my family. They trust you too. Mom said you have a pure Spirit."

"Huh, I doubt that's what she'd say right now." He squeezed me a bit tighter.

"Not that kind of Spirit. Not your Christian spirit." I gripped his arms, holding them around me. "You know a bit about the local cultures, but there's things you don't know. Especially about… my family, our tribe."

"I know the tribes have their… secrets, if you want to call them that. I figured I'd find out about them when the time came, if it was important. Is it?"

"Feels that way." The hot water had relaxed me, but there was still a deep down stirring of anxiety. My mother said he was the one, that I had to tell him everything, but I didn't know everything. I only knew one thing for sure. "My real name isn't Elizabeth Castle."

Casey didn't say anything, but I felt his body tense just a bit at my odd statement.

"It's my legal name, but not my real name. In my culture we're not allowed to reveal our true names, except to a very few. So I don't hear it often. Almost never. But I heard it tonight, while you were gone."

"I...don't... get..." The tension in his body grew, the muscles in his arms tightening, though they remained around me. "I thought you said someone sent a drink over. Did they come to the table too?"

"No, but Yazzie did, right before you got back. She called me by my real name. She said I was in danger from dark Spirits."

"Yazzie... are you sure you heard her correctly, that it wasn't some Cocopah term?"

"It's not. My mother said tribal spiritualists can get the name from their elemental Spirits. They told her and she came to warn me. And it's not just Yazzie. My mother was waiting for me to call, saying she knew I was in danger too."

"Okay. I know your mother, so I'll accept this. She knew things about me I hadn't told you yet." His arms eased a bit, as if he was shaking off his doubts. "So, if you're willing to tell me your name's not Elizabeth, are you going to tell me what it really is?"

"Din'ah."

"Dina?" Casey let out a huff. "That's not weird at all. I was expecting something strange or exotic. What about the last name?"

"It's Din-ah, not Dina, and it's Casatchellia'da. It was Americanized to Castle."

"Casta-what? That doesn't even remotely sound Navajo."

"Because I'm not Navajo either, but don't ask what I am. It's some big family secret that apparently I'm finally ready to learn. Mom told me a few things, but I need to look them up and see if I can figure any of this out before they get here."

Casey stiffened up again. "Before who gets here?"

"Everyone. My parents and my brothers. She'd already told them to come here, before I called her. She says they have to be here to help me. I don't know why, or from what, but I..." My head was starting to hurt again and I twisted around so I could lay against Casey's chest. "…it feels as if that's what is supposed to be happening. Them, and telling you."

"I'm understanding less and less of this, not more." Casey readjusted his hold on me. "You're not Beth, but Din…ah, and you're not Navajo, though that part wasn't a big surprise. No one in your family looks Navajo, no offense to the Navs. Your dad looks like one of those old pictures of Apache warriors, and I guess your brothers too. But I suppose you're not Apache."

"Yeah…no. Pretty sure we're not Apache either."

"Well, it'll be interesting to find out what you are. And why you can suddenly tell me that much. Almost as much as finding out why what happened on your run has your whole family flocking out here. This is not making sense."

"No it doesn't, but…" I wondered about telling him more, but mom had said to tell him. "…something else happened out there. Something Lutz didn't see."

"Of course!" Casey huffed, but didn't let go. "Let's get it all out."

"Okay." I shifted again, this time straddling his legs so I could see his face. Maybe a part of me didn't trust he wouldn't roll his eyes at me if I wasn't looking.

"I never really believed in all this Spirit stuff, but when that man was only about a meter away from me. I saw something floating around him, like a… ghost. Or, as it seems to be pointed out to me repeatedly, a Spirit. It was attached to him, maybe influencing him. I could see his eyes and he wasn't in the least bit worried that I had my gun pointed at his head. It, that thing, scared me more than he did."

Casey's hands stroked my legs, his eyes not betraying the slightest doubt or question that I might be somehow suffering some weird delusion. "I'm sure that would freak me out too, then everything else on top of that."

"So you're not going to say I'm crazy or was dehydrated, or heatstroke?"

"I know you. Nothing scares you, but I can feel how… disturbed, you are about this. If anyone else tried to tell me this, I'd be calling for an ambulance, but it's you. I believe everything you're telling me."

I let out a relieved sigh. He meant every word. I could see it in his eyes and started to understand what my mother called a pure Spirit. That I couldn't be with anyone else. Some of that deep down tension I'd held forever, fluttered away from me. I couldn't think of sharing this with anyone, but Casey, ever. He was part of me. He always had been. I just never let myself see it, until now.

"Oh, my love." He reached up and brushed my cheek. "It's all going to be fine." I didn't realize I'd started to cry. He pulled me back into his arms. "We'll figure this all out."

CHAPTER

8

As tired as I was after our hot bath, I had to look up the things my mother had said. Snuggled up in bed, we browsed for information on Star People, Maxa'xak and the Yahi. Most of the info was vague conjecture, research gathered by anthropologists, which meant it was only what the tribal people wanted to tell them and numerous fictions masquerading as facts about our many different cultures.

Some stories were hilarious to read, but many struck home in sad ways. Stories of the trials the Native Americans struggled through after America was 'discovered' by the white men. The Yahi story though, that was the most curious. I read a part of it out loud to Casey.

"They called him the last wild Indians."

"They haven't met your brothers…ouch" Casey grabbed my elbow. "Was he part of your secret tribe? He couldn't tell anyone his name either."

"I wouldn't think so." I went to the last known picture of him. "My mother said we failed them and from the reports, their people were completely erased in the early twentieth century. As the lone survivor, he lived out the rest of his life with no one ever knowing his name. Like my family, he wasn't allowed to tell it, though his rules were slightly different."

"Either way, it has to be a lonely existence."

Cocooned in his arms and blankets, that part of me felt less painful. Though I still felt like Beth, two people outside my family knew my Spirit name. Somehow it felt like I'd been freed from some prison. "It was."

I turned to the next stories, scanning them for clues.

"Din'ah." Casey whispered it in my ear, making me shiver. "Let's put this away for tonight. You're barely awake."

The same page on Maxa'xak myths faded as my computer pad started to time out on me. "You're right. I can't read anymore." I tapped off, sliding it onto the side table and rolling over to wrap my arms around him. "I have so much to ask my mother when she gets here."

"Well, that's not going to be for a few days." Casey leaned over me, brushing my hair back. "I know things are crazy right now, but I really missed you."

His body pressed down against me and I tightened my arms. "I missed you too and I'm sorry how I left things."

"We both have our careers to consider, but I never doubted your feelings. I knew you loved me, so I was willing to fight it out with you." He kissed me. "Now that we've jumped one hurdle, we can figure the rest of it out, together."

"I can't even begin to tell you… oh, hell." I tightened my arms around his neck. "Come here!" I pulled his head down and kissed him, getting a rumble of something between a laugh and groan as I wrapped my leg over him.

Four to five days apart always left a challenge to see how fast we could get home and out of our clothes. This time had been hampered by all the weird shit, but right now we both pushed it far out of our heads.

But it wasn't just time apart that made this reunion different. Our relationship had always run hot, but part of me held him at an arms distance. Telling him my Spirit name removed that barrier, and he felt it too. His usual slow seduction was tossed aside for a wild passion I hadn't felt since our very first time together.

We were partners for a good six months, going out on patrols, spending our days and nights together, but always strictly professional. It hadn't escaped my attention that Casey was a handsome man, by all my standards. Those deep brown eyes and long lashes had a way of distracting me. But I was a Marine and he was Border Patrol, and we had a job to do.

Then one day I slipped on a rock while checking out one of the relief stations. I had on combat boots, but the ankle twisted up anyway. I rode out the rest of the day and wrapped it up before going to sleep. Somewhere in the middle of the night I woke up screaming in pain, my whole leg cramped up.

Casey heard me and came into my room. I tried to make him go away, but my leg was in visible spasms. He disappeared for a minute and returned with his overnight kit. I was beyond protesting as he took my leg and started to massage some ointment onto it. It was cold and hot at the same time and smelled of eucalyptus. In a few minutes my leg started to feel better.

He removed the wrap from my ankle, poking around and proclaiming nothing seemed damaged, just bruised. Dehydration was the probable cause for the cramping. He made me drink down a bottle of fortified water, while he continued to gently rub my leg.

I watched him, watching me, through those luscious lashes. Did his hand linger just a bit too long? Did I lean into his touch? Whoever made that first move, some switch got flipped and there was no stopping either of us.

Getting through the rest of our patrol was almost impossible. We didn't want to leave the trailer, but had a job to do before we could return to base. When we did, we skipped the club, exchanging whispers in the parking lot on what to do next. I met him at his apartment. By the end of the month I'd moved in, unofficially.

Because we worked together, we couldn't be discovered or we'd be broken up as patrol partners, but then by the end of the year he got promoted. Our first week apart nearly killed me. I had emotions I'd never experienced with anyone else. But I held it together and got back from my first patrol with a new partner. Casey was waiting at HQ when I rolled in. He took us public with a long, hot kiss.

There was no doubt in anyone's mind by the time he let go of me that the BP Regional Commander and U.S. Marine Captain were a couple.

Now we were crossing another threshold. I could feel it. His strong arms made me feel rooted to this place, to this world. No longer an outsider simply passing through. He made me feel complete, but also filled me with a sense of dread. The stories on the internet were myths, but I had no doubt real life was going to be a lot more terrifying.

I also had no doubt Casey would stand beside me, no matter what the truth was. I ran my fingers through his hair as he finally slept, his head on my chest, his arms wrapped around me, his legs tangled with mine. I let out a single laugh, knowing he hated his hair messed up, unless it was me doing it.

He was mine. Such a pleasant thought to drift off to.

A buzzing woke us both. It felt like I'd only just closed my eyes. Casey reached for his phone as I looked at the clock. It was just a little after four in the morning. His phone was in sleep mode, except for emergency calls. This ringtone said it was critical.

Casey jabbed at the face of the phone, still blurry-eyed, hitting the call button out of habit. "Delgado here."

I got up, turning the lamp on and heading for the closet to get him a clean uniform. He grumbled through whatever they were telling him, dragging himself up. He closed the bathroom door, but I could hear him issuing orders to secure the area, call in backup from the State Police. I pulled on one of his t-shirts.

He was slicking back his hair when he came out again. "What's up?"

"Truck load of illegals." He sounded grim.

"How bad?" If they were okay, they wouldn't be making him come out to the scene.

"All dead." He shook his head as he sat on the edge of the bed to put his boots on. "Probably going to be out all day. I'll let you know." He looked over to my tablet. "It'll give you time to do some more digging."

"I'll fix you a thermos." I left him to finish getting ready. There was no point asking any more questions. If it had been on the proving grounds he'd have asked for Marine backup and I might have gone with him, but he'd ordered in the State. Still, with what was going on in the Tinajas, I wondered.

I was half-tempted to get dressed and go with him anyway, but he stepped into the kitchen as the last drops of coffee filled the thermos. He leaned down to kiss my cheek as I screwed the lid on. "Sorry I have go."

"Duty calls. I know it as well as you do." I gave him a kiss, slipped the thermos into his backpack and tossed in a couple of my MREs. "Call me when you get a chance. Keep your eyes open." I didn't know why I threw that warning in, but it felt right. "Anything look strange, stranger than it should, let me know."

The incidents at the bar were enough for Casey to take my warning seriously. "I'll keep one eye on my back."

I resisted a swipe at his hair. A regular duty day I'd have done it, but he looked so grim. Strangely it only made him more handsome. Tall, dark, brooding. A crisp uniform, starched to a razor sharpness that would make any Marine proud. He was already broad-chested, so the layer of Kevlar under his shirt only added bulk to his muscular frame. The short-sleeved summer uniform displayed just enough of his biceps to warn off anyone wanting to take him on in a tussle.

Looking at him made my whole body tingle. He was definitely mine. "I'll be waiting for you." I slipped the pack up his arm and stretched to kiss him again. "Be safe." He let me walk him out to the landing.

I lingered after he was gone. "Be safe."

CHAPTER

9

Back inside the apartment it was quiet. I started back to bed, but the call had gotten enough adrenaline going to wake me up. I grabbed my tablet and switched the pod in the coffee machine, making a pot of my favorite brew. Casey liked it strong enough to get up and walk out on its own. I preferred it mild and flavored with vanilla, with lots of cream and sugar.

I snuggled into the corner of our sofa with coffee and my tablet, taking up the topics of Maxa'xak and Star People again.

Just as it was the night before, there was nothing but a lot of Native American myths. I'd heard different versions of the story growing up, but I also remembered my father warning me and my brother that myths always had a grain of truth at their core. So, what was the truth?

After a dozen similar myths, exhaustion won out over caffeine, not that I really cared. I let myself put the tablet down and pull the fuzzy blanket over my shoulder. A few more hours of sleep wouldn't hurt.

My whole body burned, but there was no pain. The fire came from inside me. It had been there forever and was finally releasing itself, rising up through me and spreading. It was a light as blinding as the sun. I felt like the sun. I'd always enjoyed laying in the sun, absorbing the energy, becoming that energy, but now it came from inside me.

I could flow away with the light, except for a weight clinging to me. If I could only shake it loose. Opening my eyes I could see the restraint attached to me. It was the man from the mountains and our arms clung to each other in the last throws of hand-to-hand battle. He screamed as my light burned where he touched me, where I gripped his neck.

With a sweep of my leg, I tossed him to the ground, not releasing his neck as I knelt on his chest. Words flowed out of me, the secret language taught to us by my mother. It's a prayer to release the evil Spirit from its host body. The man screamed louder as the ghostly shape I'd seen possessing him writhe through him.

This was killing him, but looking down into the man's eyes, I could see he was already dead. For all the fear and pain, there was no light in those eyes, just the same deadly dark beady eyes that had stared at me in our first meeting. Once this Spirit left him, he would truly be dead. I had no choice. I pressed my knee harder into his chest, repeating the prayer slowly, firmly.

As if my words were poison, the Spirit released the man. His hands stopped prying at my arms and dropped to the sand beneath us. His neck split open and the dark Spirit flowed out onto the ground like a snake, trying to reach the safety of the rocks we fought among. I gave it no quarter, drawing my knife and driving the blade down through the Spirit. It let out a sick scream of its own, then curled into a ball around the knife, and died.

Looking down, the man stared at me still, but there was no breath, no Spirit, not even the one he'd once possessed. He had been nothing but a vessel for the evil. Now he was nothing.

Standing up, I heard more screams from somewhere higher in the mountains. Looking to the sun I felt the desire to let myself go to it, but I must find the Maxa'xak. I must end it, once and for all. I prepared myself to follow, but I am not alone. My family stood behind me, shining. Possessed by the same light of the sun. Behind them stand others. Star People. We are Star People, here to save the Earth People from this demon.

I step over the one I crushed. There is true killing that must be done.

I hit my leg on the table as I jump up from the sofa. My body felt hot, but not from the blanket. I felt a fever and saw a glow in my skin that didn't belong there. "What the hell?" I rubbed at my arms, but the iridescence remained.

"You okay?" Lutz called out from his bedroom and I heard him open the door.

"Yeah, I'm fine." I grabbed the blanket and wrapped it around me, heading for the bedroom. "Just bumped into the table. Sorry I woke you."

"You didn't." He was in the hallway as I slipped into my bedroom, closing the door. "You sure you okay? You don't have to run off. I've seen you in your jammies."

I try to laugh, dropping the blanket. The glow was gone. "Ahmmm... I need to take a shower. Help yourself to whatever you want."

"Okay. I need coffee. Mind if I change the pod? I can smell that fru-fru stuff you drink."

"Yeah, whatever you want." I checked everywhere on my arms. The fever was gone too. Going to the bathroom, I checked the mirror and pressed my hands to my face. Nothing. No heat, no glow. Just the short-breathed panic. *Did I imagine all that?*

I wanted to tell myself it was a dream, but deep down there was still that warm feeling. I yearned for it, as if it was something taken from me a long time ago and finally found again. A shower might resolve that feeling. A cold shower and then a phone call.

By the time I finished the shower, my body felt normal again, while my imagination was more convinced it was all part of the dream. I dressed and tucked my burner phone into my pocket, heading out to join Lutz.

The smell of bacon permeated the apartment and he was at the table, reading his own tablet as he crunched away on a thick crispy slice. "Made enough for two."

"Thanks." I headed into the kitchen, fixing myself a fresh cup of coffee, but skipping the cream and sugar. "Find everything you wanted?"

"And then some. Thanks for the hospitality." Lutz turned his tablet to me. "You see the news yet? Is Delgado out on this job?"

Scrambled eggs with cheese and onions, bacon, toast, our usual patrol breakfast. I loaded up a plate and joined him at the table, taking his tablet. A burned out stolen delivery truck found off Hwy 8, filled with bodies of dead illegals. "Yeah. He got called out at four this morning. Don't have any details yet."

"Shame. All our work and this still happens. Damned Coyotes." Lutz took his tablet back. "They'd have been better off coming through our corridor."

"Maybe." My instincts weren't so sure, but I didn't want to say anything right now. I restarted my tablet. Normally I spent the first morning home reviewing mission recordings for my official report. Then I'd forward it to HQ.

That was the procedure, but today was different. I had something serious to deal with. Even though the patrol leaving this morning was working the different sector, I had to say something to someone.

"Let's go over this business yesterday and then we can decide what to report."

"Happy you asked. I need to see it all again, just to know we didn't dream it all up." He smirked his doubt.

I set up my tablet, downloading the recordings and set them to play side-by-side. Lutz propped his legs on an empty kitchen chair, leaning back in his chair. Since nothing had happened the first three days, other than undisturbed relief stations, I fast-forwarded to our leaving RS4.

We reached the point where I noticed the fake brushing of tracks. The recording showed me leaving the main wash. Lutz' video still ran parallel to mine. A bouncy view of my backside. The video went through my lesson on erasing tracks.

We progressed up the wash a short distance, then my video went to static. As Lutz reached the same point in the trail, his went out too.

"Shit!" We said it in unison, sitting forward.

I re-ran the recording. Nothing. A seven minute gap of nothing, but static. I ran it frame by frame, hoping for a flicker of our assailants. It was blank until I came down the wash again, following Lutz.

"We got zip!"

Lutz pushed away from the table. "I thought it was just the radio links."

"So did I. Now it's just our word that there's something going on up there." I got up from the table, pacing. "I need a statement from you, just in case. Something we can make sure gets to our commander if anything else happens."

"Like them carrying out their threats?" Lutz crossed the room to look out over the apartment courtyard. "I didn't hear what he said to you, but I know when someone holding a gun on me is perfectly willing to pull the trigger. His backup was just waiting for the order to take us down."

"I need you to say that, for the record." I returned to the table, switching to my incident report program. "I need to report this, even if I do end up getting charged with… whatever they might dream up."

"We take our orders from the Marines and the President, not some freak in the desert." He came back to the table, picking up his own tablet. "I'll record whatever you need."

"Just the facts. What you witnessed, not what I told you."

CHAPTER 10

I remained at the table, opening an incident report, uploading our mission videos and filling in the missing seven minute gap. I could repeat the encounter nearly verbatim, right down to the last warnings. I wrapped it up with the suspicious marks under my vehicle and the threatening drink delivered to my table.

Lutz returned from his room. I didn't look up at him, instead focused on the camera's eye. "A statement from Sgt. Brandon Lutz is attached to my own, but I feel it is necessary to return to the site, legitimately sanctioned or not, to confirm their presence is not in violation of military regulations. This report will be electronically delivered in three days if I do not return to deliver or rescind it personally."

Lutz' mouth was open, but he didn't interrupt me. Not until I uploaded his statement and shut down the video. "You plan on going back out there?"

I hadn't consciously thought about it until the words came out of my mouth. "Every fiber in my body is screaming that something is wrong out there. Wrong on a universal scale. I can't just hope someone else investigates. I have to do this."

"No! We have to. You're not going out there alone. I'm your partner."

"I can't ask you to stick your neck out."

"I'm going and I'm sure your boyfriend…"

"Absolutely not!" I stood up, leaning over the table. "You're not saying anything to him. That's an order."

Lutz took a step back at my sudden vehemence. In our few months as partners I'd never forced an order. I could see him struggle with it, then nod. "Yes, ma'am, but I'm going with you, or I will be forced to report you to our unit commander."

He didn't flinch as I squinted back at him. *Touché*. "All right, Sgt. Get ready. Pull whatever supplies we'll make travel arrangements." He headed to his room and I sent the report to my private cloud account, set it to automatically broadcast one hour after we were scheduled to report back to duty.

Using my burner phone, I set my plan into motion. Within an hour a neighbor drove us out of the complex, Lutz and I were in the back of her SUV where the windows were shaded dark against the desert sun.

Michelle looked at us in the rear-view mirror. "You sure you want to go out today? It's supposed to be well over 110 degrees."

"Only get so many days off." I kept the details limited. "We saw an interesting quartz outcrop that begs closer inspection." We were dressed in our BDU pants, boots and t-shirts, but had safety vests and backpacks of water and 'tools'. We carried our sidearms and I had an old camera attached to my belt loop, making us look all the more touristy.

"Well, Billy said just to bring the bikes back with full tanks and he's fine."

"Appreciate it. We'd have used ours, but Casey went out early this morning and I forgot to ask him for the keys. God only knows when he'll get home."

"Oh, yeah!" She looked at me in the mirror again. "I read all about it this morning. What's with people these days, killing all those innocent people? Really, I mean, yeah, they were trying to get into the country illegally, but to die like that. Then someone set them on fire." She shivered and shook her head, looking out her side window as she turned the corner. "When's all this crazy going to end?"

"Not soon enough. We'd love to be put out of work." I watched where she went, looking out for any vehicles following us. I fidgeted with the little rock Yazzie gave me, until I saw Lutz watching. I shoved it into my pocket.

It was only a few blocks to the RV Park the complex leased for residents. It kept our toys from making the parking lot look 'trashy'. The gates opened to her security code and she took us to the enclosure assigned to her family. Billy's truck, three adult desert bikes and two kids' 4-wheelers.

Lutz loaded up two of the bikes while she gave me the truck keys and her security code. "Drop the keys in the flower pot tonight and I'll get them in the morning."

"Gotcha. Maybe we'll find some pretty rocks for your pots."

"Me too?" Michelle's twelve-year old daughter leaned over the steering wheel.

"Yeah, Carly, I'll try to find you something special."

She grinned, disappearing back inside the vehicle.

"Thanks." Michelle climbed up into her SUV and waved as she exited the yard. We finished prepping the bikes.

Baseball caps, aviator glasses, shaded windows up and air conditioner cranked to full, I took us to Hwy 8. This section of the range was down for maintenance this week, so getting approval was easy.

I bypassed the range road, heading for one of the old herding trails. It wouldn't be easy. The trails were broken down, sections washed out or blocked by rock slides. If not for 4-wheel drive, we wouldn't have gotten far after we left the highway.

Lutz huffed as we bounced. "Why are we going in this way?"

"Because this is how the locals get in." I gripped the wheel as we tilted over a small slide of rocks. "Pretty obvious if we came in on the range road."

"Yeah…" He braced. "I think this is rougher than going off-road." He pointed to the side of the trail.

"Probably, but we don't damage more than we have to."

"It's a bombing range!"

I rolled my eyes at his point, valid as it was. "Yes, but it's still owned by the Cocopah."

He huffed again at a rough wash out, maybe a bit louder than normal, for emphasis.

I ignored him, sticking to the remnants of the road. It took longer to reach the trail I'd mapped out. "There's the box canyon where we can hide the truck." I pulled in, parking Billy's old beat up truck up under a mesquite tree.

Lutz cringed at a scrapping noise. "Sure he won't complain about scratches?"

I could see the limb on the hood, but shrugged. "Did you look at the truck as you loaded it? He's way past worrying about a shiny paint job." I shoved the keys down between the seats and cracked the window a few inches. "Get the bikes."

Lutz cracked his window and got out, thumping around as he unload the truck. I located the trail and rejoined him. We went over the map before mounting up.

The route wasn't any more than goat and sheep trails. The local tribes turned their herds loose here when monsoons made the desert plants grow wild. A little water and the ravines turned into beautiful gardens. Those plants changed the flavor of the goats' milk and meat.

The tribes coordinated mission and grazing dates and pilots learned fast the retribution if they went off track and shot up a herd of goats. However, sheep and goats wandered where they wanted, so it was deemed a no-foul if they grazed over the line.

Right now their four-legged paths were our way in. We tangled our way up steep ravines and through narrow passes, until I could see the flags for RS4 and RS5. I pointed them out to Lutz.

Not far off trail was a decent-sized Torote tree. Fed off whatever little bit of rain that trickled down the steep hill behind it, it provided some shade during the worst heat of the day. We tucked the bikes behind the tree and took a water break for ourselves.

Lutz sat under the tree, wiping sweat off his neck. The helmet wasn't the high-tech model we wore on duty. It had ventilation, but no fans to cool our heads. "Think we made it in undetected?"

"No guarantees." I joined him, giving the tree a token of our thanks with a splash of water before I took my own drink. Lutz remembered and gave his own offering, humoring my ritual teachings. I took a second drink. "I don't see any tampering with the path, but they wouldn't expect anything but animals to come up this way."

"Let's hope." He took one more drink before putting his bottle away. "Where now?"

I pulled out the map. "We go on foot along this ridge. It will give us cover." I pointed to an area on the aerial map of the range. "That's Surveyors Tank, RS5 and the wash we went down." My finger settled into an area between the three. "I suspect this point is where we need to go. This trail will bring us up over the top of that target."

"Huh, looks like a step carved into the side of the mountain."

"A perfect point to hide without us picking them up on satellite updates, unless we were looking for them." I folded up the map and checked my camera. It was an old digital model, not hooked up to any com lines that could be hacked. "Let's get up there."

CHAPTER

11

This wasn't our first hiking adventure. I'd been putting Lutz through my own desert survival training and he was learning. We took breaks, but the last half-hour the most brutal with an almost vertical ascent. We set rappel ropes for our descent. Fortunately the path was fairly level the rest of the way. Twenty more minutes and I pulled Lutz down behind a boulder.

"Here we are." I'd caught the briefest glimpse before taking cover. We both edged up enough again to see past this outcropping of rocks. Sure enough, on a plateau below us were buildings mashed up against the cliff face. Set in a point of almost perpetual shade. "Got'em."

We dropped back down. "I need to get pictures without them seeing me. See that brush, break me off some of the branches and drag them up here."

"Yes, ma'am!" Lutz skidded down the incline. At this altitude the shrubs didn't get much water, so they grew short and sparse. He broke off some of the branches, paying for them with the remains of a bottle of water, before he dragged them back to me. I built an impromptu blind, getting into place as Lutz pulled the last branch over us. He hung onto it as I raised my head over the rocks again.

"There's no activity." I started clicking pictures of the buildings. "One building looks rather large and newer than the other one. The second one looks reminiscent of an old miner's shack, or a mine entrance, a bit dilapidated. Two SUVs are parked up next to the cliff, but no people."

"Well, we know there are at least three trucks, so one is out here somewhere. Probably taking their bad-ass show on the road again." Lutz had a tad of snark in his tone.

"I'd rather know exactly where they.... hey, door's opening." I poised the camera, waiting. Sure enough, several men came out of the larger building, walking out into the sunlight. They were looking up, but not at us. That made me stop taking pictures and try to see what they were looking for. "Shit, hang onto the branches."

Over the opposing ridge the rotors of a helicopter appeared, running silent. I also grabbed branches of our cover, dropping my head behind the ridge. The backwash from the rotor blades hit us and it took everything to hang onto our little bit of cover.

When the turbulence stopped I slipped up to the edge again, switching my camera to video mode. "People are getting out of the helicopter. A lot of people, but from the looks of things they aren't here voluntarily."

"Illegals?" Lutz was still holding the branches, but turned enough to see the screen of my camera as I recorded the scene.

I could see the passengers now. “Yup. Looks like they’re rounding them up.”

“For what? They’re not Border Patrol and we took care of all the local vigilante groups.” He stretched to look over the edge too. Just then a woman was tossed from the helicopter, landing on her hands and knees, crying out as one of the uniformed men dragged her to the lineup. “That’s not good.” He looked over the group as they clustered together. “No kids. Where are the kids?”

I didn’t answer. I didn’t want to guess because my mind went to the darkest place ever. I kept recording as the last of the illegals were pushed into the group. That’s when I saw the man from the wash, the Smirker, walking out of the mine shack. His mouth moved, but we were too far away to hear what he said with the helicopter blades still whirling down.

“What could he possibly want with these people? Human trafficking?” Lutz caught his breath as a young man made a break from the group, running for the edge of the plateau, one of the uniforms started after him, but Smirker raised a gun. No warning shot. Hitting the man in the back.

“Shit, shit, shit…” This was definitely no government operation. Lutz looked just as horrified as I felt. The Smirker was yelling now.

I could hear him as he raised his voice. “Anyone else?” His gun was pointed at them. “There’s no escape!” He shouted it in Spanish, making sure they understood.

Just then the door to the miner’s shack opened again. I thought it was going to be more mercenaries, but I nearly dropped the camera at the sight of a large… monster slithered out onto the plateau. A large horned serpent.

"What the fuck is that?" Lutz' whole body stiffened as if ready to take off, even though we had to be at least fifty feet above the plateau.

I wanted to run too, but couldn't. That certainty that I had to come here today was vindicated. I was here to prepare myself for something bigger, something of legends. I'd seen this beast in our ancient texts, in myths told to scare children around the campfire. In the stories I'd reread only hours ago. It was alive in front of me.

"It's a..." Just thinking the word ignited a fire inside me. "It's a Maxa'xak."

"A what, a Maxak? How the fuck would you know?"

"A Maxa'xak. I'll try to explain...later." I refocused the camera.

The monster undulated across the rock floor, just as a snake would. It was easily the length of a city bus and the girth of two, three large men. Where it traveled there was a path of wet slime, but there was something wrong with the appearance. As solid as it appeared, there was a blurriness, a lack of definition.

I squeezed my eyes shut. Simple logic should have me denying what I saw, but I knew with a certainty this monster was real. I knew this monster deep down in the bones of my people. My blood burned as I reopened my eyes to look at it again. Now my vision was clear.

This was a Maxa'xak!

The beast rose up as it reached the cowering illegals, who screamed in terror, dropping to their knees as the massive horned head hovered over them. It hissed, fangs exposed and dripping as it sniffed at them. The Maxa'xak's head jerked forward and grabbed one of the men in its mouth.

He screamed in pain and terror as the giant snake carried him away. A woman dared to chase after him, but got the butt of a rifle to her head. Gun barrels started to poke at the rest of the group, urging them to their feet and herding them into the mine.

I stopped recording as the door closed, sliding down the ridge to where Lutz had escaped, throwing up over a boulder. He went into dry heaves as I rubbed his back.

"We got to get out of here."

"We can't leave them here, to that… that monster. What the hell was that?" He got his water bottle out and tried to take a drink, a small one.

"The horned serpent. An evil water Spirit."

"Seriously?" He looked at me as if I was crazy. "It's got to be alien."

I could see he was reaching past his own beliefs to come up with an explanation. "I guess you could call it that, but they've been here for as long as we have. A lot longer than even my people." I heard the words coming out of my mouth, but I didn't know why. I just knew they were true.

"We have to go." I turned back to the ridge, pulling down the branches and starting to erase our presence. "Bury that." I pointed to the bile he'd spewed.

He nodded, looking around for a pile of dirt or sand he could use, being careful in case we hadn't already scared off any resident snakes. Somehow I had the feeling they were long gone. They were as much a part of the Earth as all the other natural critters. That monster wasn't. They'd get as far away from this cursed place as possible.

Lutz covered his mess, then mimicked my ground beating to hide his scuffs. He looked to me for approval and I gave it to him, letting him take the lead down the mountain as I swept up behind us. Getting down the cliff was a lot faster, both of us motivated by fear. We took no breaks until we reached the bikes.

Lutz was gasping, trying to get a drink, spilling more water than went down his throat. "You said that was a water spirit. In case you didn't notice, there's no fucking water here. What the fuck is that thing doing here? And how do you know what the fuck it is?"

I couldn't blame him for being freaked out. "I don't know. I mean I do, but I don't have time to run down all the Native American Spirits for you, so welcome to my world. Now let's get the fuck out of here. Okay?"

CHAPTER 12

I threw my leg over my bike and helmeted up, triggering the motor, making sure it was still in street-mode. It ran quieter, which right now I desperately wanted as we made our escape. I rolled forward, but waited as Lutz mounted up.

We made down to the next ridge when there was a sudden puff of dust just ahead of us. “Shit!” I swung my bike off course, several more dust clouds appeared where I’d just been. I gunned it over the top of the ridge, Lutz nearly slamming into me as he cleared it too.

I slowed only long enough to shout at him. “Stick close if you can, otherwise, that is your target, west side.” I pointed to a distinctive ridge above where we’d parked the truck. I got a single nod and took off again.

This wasn’t the route we’d taken coming in, but we had no choice. We had to get out of here before it got dark or we’d have to ditch the bikes and walk out. A part of me thought we would have to anyway, if we wanted to really lose these guys.

I held off on that decision, continuing along the opposite side of the ridge, using it as cover, but trying to keep my body down against the body of the bike.

Until they crested the ridge, they couldn't shoot at us again, unless they came after us with the helicopter. The further we got out of the mountains, the less likely they'd risk following us. Getting into open airspace opened them up to being picked up by range surveillance. The range guys hated errant flyboys and wouldn't hesitate to call in air support.

We had to reach those foothills. Fast.

Sticking to the ridge gave us cover, but it also opened us up to another risk. A curve around a large boulder brought us to the area I dreaded most. I'd avoided it on our way in because the goat path here ran right along a cliff edge.

I stopped, looking up to see if we had anyone tailing us yet. "Hate to do this, but we have no choice. Be careful and stick to the path. If we have to ditch, go for the wall and be ready to shoot it out."

"Yes, ma'am!" He patted the strap of the rifle slung over his shoulder.

I gave a glance down the cliff face, nearly three hundred feet straight down, maybe deeper with the graveyard of rock slides and gaping ravine at the bottom. Looking forward I pinpointed three strategic points where we had cover, pointing them out to Lutz. With a nod I took off, Lutz giving me room to navigate the narrow path.

We made it to the first outcrop of rock, pausing to check the ridge and taking off to the next point. A boulder the size of a house left only enough room for us to squeeze our bikes through. From there to the third point the path was a bit wider. I revved it and took off.

Almost to the end of the cliff trail I felt something graze my leg and my control panel exploded. I tried to swerve for the wall, but my tire blew and I skidded out. As I rolled off into rocks, my bike hit a crevice and somersaulted straight off the cliff. I hit the wall as bullets hit Lutz. I saw the back of his helmet shatter and his body stiffened, the swerve of the bike carried him over the edge before I could scream.

Stunned, I laid there for a second, then remembered we were being hunted. I pushed up and got my bearings. I couldn't stay here. They'd come this way to make sure we were dead. Against the wall I was covered by an outcropping cut out by rain and wind.

I stuck to it, backtracking to the second checkpoint, the huge boulder. It nearly blocked the path, but there was a gap on this side. A spot just big enough for me to squeeze into it. I had to remove my backpack to fit through.

There was more room inside. Water had washed out some of the rock behind the crevice, creating a cave, letting me disappear completely. I dropped my backpack and slid down the wall. I felt the little rock in my pocket, taking it out and squeezing it tight in one hand, my gun in the other. Just then I heard the familiar sound of rattling.

"Really?" Squinting my eyes in the dark shadows of the makeshift cave, I saw a huge rattler coiled up, staring back at me. Any other time I'd consider shooting it, but that wouldn't work, so I stared back at it. "Just fucking bite me and get it over with." It was a whisper, in the language I nearly never spoke.

The snake stopped rattling and dropped its defensive posture.

Ok…kay. Instinct rose up in me. I pulled my water bottle out and poured water onto the cave floor. It trickled down towards the snake. Miraculously, it stopped watching me, its flickering tongue lapping up the offering. "Thank you." I whispered to the snake.

Leaning my head against the wall, the last few minutes replayed in my head. Lutz was dead and I was hiding in a cave with a rattlesnake as my new best friend. This was not how I'd seen this going. What was I going to tell Sabrina, his family? Silent tears trickled down my cheeks.

A little rattle from the snake got my attention. It faced the opening of our cave. I didn't move, but the snake did, slithering closer to the entrance and recoiling. She didn't take her eyes off the one way into our hideout.

"Dis' it. There's da guy." Someone slurred with a terrible southern accent.

"And his bike, wait… there's the other bike. I told you I got her." The other voice was without an accent.

"Guess ya did. I's sure she cleared da cliffs." I heard a hard slap.

"Damn you! Shove me again and you'll join our friends down there." There was some grumbling and more cursing. Laughter. Maybe four guys? "I got her, but I don't see her body down there."

"Could be in d'hole, but we betta search. Boss'll toss ya into dat pit if ya wrong."

"Yeah, both of us. You two, head on down the path. I hit her, so she'd be bleeding. Get back here before it gets dark. We need to be over the ridge for our extraction."

Hearing that, I looked down and saw blood on my leg. The shock of hitting the wall, then seeing Lutz die, must have blurred it out. I was bleeding, but not enough to leave a trail.

"Too bad they came back sticking their nose into our business. Jeeters said he was sure those papers would keep their mouths shut, backed up by sending them those threats."

"Dey didn't talk, or we'd be worr'in bout all kinda soldiers up in here."

"Still, while no one's going to miss the Mexicans, two Marines are another story. That Border Patrol officer is going to suspect they came back."

"Itza lot of moun'ins and dey din come up da wash. Dey won't find us. And dat loada bodies got dumped miles from ere. Maxi's gotta a'hole new batch ta play with. Nough for us ta hold out until the army gives up."

"If they find our friends down there, they'll find bullet holes in them."

"Won't be no bodies if furred co'otes get'em. If na, da two-leg kind get blamed. We jus gotta lay low." The speaker gave a sigh. "Shame, mighta been fun keep'n her round."

"Yeah, like the boss would let that happen." The other speaker laughed. "I was standing behind him and saw the look in her eyes. She's the dangerous kind."

"An' we not?"

"Man, when someone stops asking questions, they're ready to shoot. If Jeeter'd flinched, she'd have plugged him, me and probably a few more before we got her. If we got her." He let out a sigh. "And I saw the tat on her arm. A

Raider Cross with hash-marks, Special Forces with recorded kills. Nothing sweet under the skin of that dame."

I couldn't help but be a bit impressed that he saw my tattoo and knew what it meant. Few people outside the Marines did. And he'd been right. I now wished I had gone for the shootout.

"Come on, we better look around a bit more before the team gets back."

"Ya right. She's a lil thang and dey some big ho's round ere."

I tensed, knowing this was the only place big enough to hide me. My friendly snake hadn't relaxed at all, still poised by the slit between cliff and wall. *Strange*. Since I could walk I'd been taught to respect the creatures around me, but until now it had been only a lesson. Now those teachings were proving to be something more, something spiritual. A connection.

The snake raised its head and tail.

"Hey, we gotta ho'!" The southern voice boomed into the little cave. I pressed as far into the notch as I could.

"Well, see if she's in there." The other man was a distance away.

"You look. I hate ho's."

"You big pussy." The other man sounded closer. "Get out of the way."

Just then my snake hissed and rattled its tail. I saw its head bolt towards the opening.

"Shit! Son of a bitch!" Both men swore at the same time.

"Damn fucking thing nearly got me." I heard the click of a safety being released.

"Man, ya stupid? Ain't nothing in dat ho' but da snake."

"We don't know that. Draw it out and I'll shoot it."

My snake rattled more vehemently, but this time it wasn't alone. I heard at least three more, though I couldn't see them.

"FUCK NO! Da's a whole nest of'em in der."

I found it wildly ironic he was afraid of snakes, considering what he worked for.

"Okay, okay, back away." Both sounded scared now. "She didn't go in there."

My snake and her friends rattled a few more times, then stopped, but she remained vigilant. I looked upwards. It was dark, but there were more notches in the wall. Clearly this was a favorite spot for them. Maybe a real nest. Arizona Diamondbacks were known to stay with their young, and co-parent with other females.

I went back to being nervous, sitting in the middle of a snake nursery, though they didn't seem to care I was there. It was over a half-hour before the rest of the team returned saying they saw no sign of footprints or blood. Finally they all agreed I was at the bottom of the cliff too.

My friend relaxed her pose again, returning to a depression in the ground. Probably her nest. I waited another ten minutes before daring to shift positions, I slowly opened my backpack and using the flashlight on my phone, got a look at the cave.

Other snakes were there, watching me, but not taking a defensive posture. Along one section of the wall I saw trickle marks where rainfall ran down the walls to collect on the floor. Monsoons would start soon, but it was dry in the cave.

Tucking Yazzie's little rock into my bra, where it would be touching my skin, I sang a prayer as I sacrificed one of my bottles of water. A tribute for the help they'd given me. I built a rock nest against the wall, making sure I could get the bottle up to one of the trickle marks.

The bottle fit snug in the rocks. I cut a hole in it big enough for a snake's head to reach inside for water, pinching the flap back again the wall to create a funnel. It would give them a few days water now and maybe something of a well for the future.

"I thank your Earth Spirits for saving my life." I put everything away and eased past my lethal friend to the entrance. She acted as if I wasn't even there, as did the others.

CHAPTER

13

Out in the open air again, I stuck to the boulder, listening for footsteps on the cliff path. They must have really believed me dead. I reached the point that had been just narrow enough for us to squeeze our bikes through. Looking around the boulder I saw no one. They were gone.

I took a deep breath before looking down.

If I hadn't seen him die the second his helmet shattered, the fall would have finished the job. I dropped to my knees. Momentum had carried Lutz a ways from the cliff edge, thrown into a section where rockslides had created a slope. He laid tangled, limbs broken and twisted in unnatural positions.

"I'm sorry. I shouldn't have let you come with me. I should have lied to you. I should have waited." I whispered it down to Lutz, letting tears fall into the same void.

A wind blew up the face of the cliff, carrying with it a sound like crying. Coyotes, but it wasn't their usual voice as they went out on the hunt. This was mournful. "Oh, please. Leave him alone until I can come back for him."

As if in spite of my plea, a large coyote came up out of the ravine, slowly approaching Lutz' body.

No, no, no… I wanted to scream down the cliff to scare it off, but our assailants might hear me. Two more coyotes followed the first. I crawled over to loose rocks piled against the boulder, returning to the edge. I started to take aim, but the sight stopped me.

More of the pack had reached Lutz' body. They encircled it, laying down next to him. The large coyote sat at his head, keening that sad song. I put down the rocks and answered with a song, a prayer of protection. The coyote keened louder in response, his eyes directly on me.

Looking at my hands planted on the ground, I caught my breath. They glowed, just as they had this morning after my weird dream. All the coyotes gazed at me, letting out soft howls. "Take care of my friend. I'll be back for him."

The keening stopped and the large coyote laid down, resting his head on Lutz' shoulder. I could barely believe what I was watching as the shadows of the mountains around us grew darker. Night would be here soon.

I hated to leave, but there was nothing I could do for Lutz. Except live long enough to come back and avenge him. My hands glowed brighter with the thought. My whole body did. It should have scared me. This wasn't natural, but neither was the Maxa'xak.

I slipped back to the wall. I certainly didn't need anyone noticing a walking glow stick.

I had to move. Just because those men didn't find me, or my body, didn't mean they wouldn't come back looking for me as it got darker. They had a helicopter to look for illegals. It probably had heat-seeking infrared equipment, radar-jammers, all kinds of technology. A body retained heat for several hours, enough to be detected. They'd be able to find me dead or alive in the dark, which was coming fast.

Reaching a point where the path dropped down off the shelf, I heard a sound behind me. I dropped, expecting to be jumped on by the men. Instead beady eyes caught the remaining light. More coyotes.

I stared back for a moment. "Well, as the animal Spirits are clearly siding with me today, are you here to help me?" The coyotes moved forward, heads down, no teeth bared. "Okay. I need to get to my truck."

I got up slowly and started back to the original path, as it was the safest descent. The coyotes trotted along after me, as if nothing more than domestic shepherds. I found the goat track, a few minutes later the sun disappeared completely.

Using my flashlight, I could see by the shadows we were getting close to the foothills. I felt relief, until I heard a yipping from one of the coyotes. A light crested the ridge. I looked for a hole, but there was nothing but a couple bushes.

I switched off the flashlight and tried to crawl between them. Next thing I knew one of the coyotes grabbed my hand, hard enough to keep me from jerking away, but not enough to break the skin. It pulled down. Instinct told me to obey.

I curled up on the ground and the pack swarmed me. The big guy who'd pulled me down climbed on top my back. Others crowded around me. The helicopter's lights hit us. I kept my head down and limbs folded up. The pack started howling, growling and yapping at the helicopter. I hoped I looked like one of the coyotes, or downed prey.

Must have. After about fifteen more seconds the helicopter continued down the path, staying close to ground level to avoid air traffic control picking them up. I peeked up from the cluster, draping my arms over the backs of the pack. At the bottom of the mountain the helicopter swung back our way, but the searchlight was off. I stayed put until it veered into the nearest mountain ravine and disappeared.

Way out on the flat of the desert I saw bright lights moving in a pattern northwards. Range maintenance teams? They'd be heading in. My enemies would want to avoid them. I remained with my canines another few minutes and got several licks to the face. I hugged the two I was clinging onto, my body emitting a soft glow with their loving. "Thank you, really."

I got more face licks from the others before a few of them took off down the path ahead of me. Scouting the way. The rest stayed with me. I let them lead me. The path frequently forked out into other paths, but they kept me on the one with bike tracks still in the dirt. As the moon crested the mountains, we reached the little canyon where I'd hidden the truck.

The coyotes danced about as I threw all my stuff in the truck. I pulled out a pack of beef jerky Lutz had packed for our snacks. We'd never got around to it. There were a couple bottles of water in the truck. In the back was a hubcap Billy always complained fell off at every pot hole. I laid it on the ground and poured all my water into it.

The coyotes lapped it up. There were hidden pools in the mountains and Surveyors Tank actually had a trough set up, but they'd earned my tribute. While they drank I opened the jerky. Smelling meat, they left the water after getting their laps and circled me. "So now I'm a coyote whisperer too?"

Of course they didn't answer. They were salivating over the bag. I gave them each a chunk and they trotted off into the dark, happy with their rewards. "Mom, you got a lot of explaining to do."

As much as I wanted to call her, I had to get my ass out of here. I tossed my backpack into the seat next to me as I got into the truck. The empty seat. A wave of grief boiled up again, but I had to keep under control. I had to get off the range.

Instead of giving in, I pulled my spare pistol out, the standard issue Beretta M9, double-checking the safety and shoving it between the seats where I could reach it in an instant. From my holster I removed my Sig Sauer 226 and jammed it in front of the Beretta. They'd stay put on the rough roads. I shifted the truck into gear and pulled out from behind the tree.

I couldn't turn my lights on, not yet, but the moon was nearly full and the sky clear, lighting the desert enough for me to guess where the remains of the old road were. Going slow, the bouncing wasn't as bad, but it wore on me. My leg hurt. After four or five miles I pulled my burner phone out and stuck it into the phone holder Billy installed on the dash. I pressed the auto-call for Casey.

Immediately he picked up. "Where the hell are you?"

"Lutz is dead. They killed him."

"Are you all right? Where are you?" He still sounded pissed, but concerned.

"We had to go back and take a look. I'm sorry." I grunted through a washed out section of the road, bouncing. "I'm about ten miles southeast of Butler pass. I'm going to try to take the old range road from there back to the maintenance road. You gotta meet me. I'm in Billy's truck. Please hurry."

"Are you hurt?" Casey said it louder, slower.

"I'm… I got grazed along my leg, but there's something going on. I can't explain it. Just meet me."

"I'll be there." He wasn't shouting at me. "What else can I do?"

My mind jumped around. I was tired. Way more tired than I should be. "Just be there, please." Off to my left I could see the splattering reflection the moonlight made against the foothills of the Butler Mountains. "I love you."

"I love you too. Be careful."

I disconnected before he said anything else. Focusing my eyes on this dark road.

A pass ran between the Butler Mountains. An old range road from back in the twentieth century. There was a radar installation up there for training the pilots to avoid Triple-A and SAM missiles.

Now there was a goat herder hut. A little pre-fab structure they used when they had free run of the range during the spring. If I had to stop, that was where Casey would come looking for me.

I didn't want to stop. Another mile or two. I just had to find the trail that connected the two ranges.

It wasn't so hard in the moon-splashed desert. A pile of rocks made the marker. The clock on the dash said it was nearly ten at night, meaning it had taken me over an hour to drive twelve miles.

I turned at the marker and was immediately rewarded by a smoother road. Not a lot smoother, but the locals did their best to fill in areas that washed out every monsoon. I wasn't being jolted so hard that the only thing preventing a concussion was my seatbelt. I gave the old truck more fuel and started the climb into the pass. If I could get over the top of it, I could turn my lights on.

I made it to the top of the pass and slid over onto the other side. I waited just a few more minutes, then flipped on my lights. I couldn't believe I'd gotten so far. They must have really thought I was dead. Maxi was going to be really pissed when I came back to kill him.

CHAPTER

14

I cringed at making light of the creature that came out of that building. Maxa'xak. A tap of another auto-call got my mother. "Who and what is Maxa'xak?"

"They are our blood enemy." I expected her to put me off, but she kept talking. "You learned the legends of a giant snake rising from the water to eat people. They are destroyers, possessors. For centuries upon centuries the Star People have pursued them, one by one, fulfilling our one true duty. To kill them and protect the People."

Two days ago I would have laughed. "It's still a fu…nasty giant snake" I caught myself from swearing. Even several hundred miles away, her tongue-lashing could be as painful as the real thing. "Those guys we ran into yesterday are abducting the illegals and giving them to him. I saw it for myself. What is he, really?"

"You went back? You were supposed to wait for your brothers." Now mom sounded scared and angry. "Did it see you? Did those men see you?"

"Yes, I… I got away, but they think I'm dead at the bottom of a ravine, next to… my friend." My voice cracked. "Mom, what's going on?"

"If they're with him, they're not men. Not anymore. Wherever you are, get somewhere safe. Your brothers left Dateland about fifteen minutes ago. Don't do anything else until they're with you. Do you hear me, Din'ah?"

So much for skipping the tongue lashing.

"Yes, mom, I hear you." A part of me was mad. I was nearly thirty, a Marine. I didn't need them rescuing me, another part of me was relieved they were close. "Mom, why am I glowing?"

"Oh my god, this is happening too fast." Now she sounded frightened instead of angry.

"Mom!" I yelled at the phone to get her attention as she rambled to herself.

"Okay…" She yelled back at me. "It's part of your Rising, Din'ah. Your Spirit sensed the danger you're in and has awakened. Don't fight it, but don't go chasing the Maxa'xak until you can fully summon her." She sounded almost panicked. "Don't do anything else until I get there. Your father will be here in an hour and we'll head that way. Don't reveal yourself to those men!"

I glanced at the time displayed on the phone. Eleven. She'd not get here until four in the morning. Daylight would be around five. "I can't promise anything, Mom. I have a duty to do something. My friend is still… Mom, coyotes are guarding his body. Rattlesnakes protected me when I climbed into their den. What's all that?"

She hesitated and I could hear her taking a deep breath. "There's not time to fully explain, but they recognized you as one of the Star People. They will protect your friend." She sighed. "I'll explain everything tomorrow. I love you, Din'ah."

"No, mom, don't hang up! I'm tired and I'm... scared. I need to stay awake. It's at least an hour before Casey finds me." I reached out, turning the phone volume up. "Tell me all the secrets you've been keeping from me."

She did. "You know the ancient myths of Star People. The Ci'inkwia. Sometimes called Thunderbirds. And of Maxa'xak, the dark horned serpent Spirit. They went by different names too, with many tribes across the country."

"Ciinkwia. I've heard those stories too. But the myths didn't always describe the Thunderbirds as too nice either. They seemed to arbitrarily kill people."

"No. Those we killed were humans the Maxa'xak used to serve as hosts for its young. They were no longer alive. The first thing the larvae did was eat into their brains and nervous systems, taking over the bodies. The Ci'inkwia can sensed the monster under human flesh. That's what happened to you. That 'ghost' you saw possessing that man."

"Jeeters. He's in charge of the men, or whatever they are."

"His evil Spirit was strong enough to force the Rising of your Star Spirit, which means it is close to maturity. A new Maxa'xak is almost ready to leave its host.

"Mom, how many of these things are around?"

"How many men did you see?"

"Eight the first time, but there could be more."

Mom let out a worried groan. "Few larvae actually live to maturity, which is why they're abducting illegals."

I counted in my head. "That's horrific. Casey went out on a call about a truckload of illegals dumped in a stolen truck. It was these same men… monsters. I think there might also be one or two on the base. They knew things they shouldn't."

"No. The young can't be separated by more than thirty miles from the parent. They're telepathically linked to regulate their growth. Longer than a day of separation the larva starts to consume their host, very quickly. I'm talking zombie-flesh boils and peeling."

"Zombies." In my head I saw her shiver. "Guess that's why you never liked us watching those movies. You saw this happen?"

"When I was a teenager. Up in Chino Valley. My mother's Spirit warned us of danger. We tracked down a young man and tried to find out where the nest was. He rotted right before my eyes. The larva tried to flee, but my father killed it."

"You saw all this, with your own eyes."

"Yes. It triggered my Rising." She sighed. "We've been tracking this one forever, but could never pinpoint the nest. I'm not strong enough to purge a Maxa'xak anymore. Now it will be your job. That is what I need to teach you."

"And you've kept this secret all these years. Why?"

Again there was a pause on the other end of the phone. A sigh. "Would you have believed any of this?"

Hell no! I kept my lips pressed together, my flesh no longer glowed hot, but was still a bit luminescent. “Probably not. So they followed us back to the base.”

“Probably.” She paused for only a second. “These evil Spirits can be persuasive in nature. When that man was warning you, he was trying to influence your human Spirit, not realizing you’re one of us.”

“Wait…” Her words rattled around my tired brain. By now I was near the maintenance road. “My human Spirit? You said I was Star People, Thunderbirds? Mom…” I hesitated to ask the crazy question that popped into my head, but I could hear Lutz asking. “Are we… human?”

She laughed. “Yes, dear Din’ah, for all intents and purposes, we’re human.”

“Mom, that’s not an answer!”

“Sorry, your dad is here. Got to go.” The light on the phone flickered, the line disconnected.

“What the fuck kind of answer is that?” I screamed at the phone, but of course got no answer.

CHAPTER

15

I almost flew over the maintenance road completely as I hit the embankment of the raised road. I braked and slid to a stop, grabbing my shoulder where the seatbelt locked and bit in enough to knock the wind out of me. "Jesus Christ."

Breathe. I forced myself to relax enough for the seatbelt to release me. I'd have a mark from that one. My pistols had shifted a bit. I put the Beretta away, but kept my Sig within reach. I looked back the way I'd come.

It was dark, no sign of headlights or search beams. Looking ahead I saw a long straight road, graded nearly as smooth as a highway. I shoved the pedal all the way to the floor.

I knew this road like the back of my hand. At night it was eerie. The bright summer moon created odd shadows in the desert, not helped by my imagination. After my mother's stories, images were running rampant in my head.

All I wanted was to get to the highway and to Yuma. To Casey. *Where was he?*

Suddenly lights appeared ahead, coming my direction. There was a curve in the road, I remembered that. About halfway to the highway. "Please be Casey, please be Casey…" *Please*. My eyes shifted to my Sig. It could also be range patrol. They'd know who was supposed to be out here, or not. I could slide, but not Casey. *Did they stop him?*

The other vehicle's headlights were up high. There were additional runner lights. Range Cops? I stopped. So did they. Headlights to headlights. I knew the cop rule. Don't move, don't get out until told to. The driver and passenger doors opened. *Damn*. Cops or bad guys? I had one hand on my Sig.

The driver stepped into the lights and my heart stuttered from racing to almost stopping. I threw open the door and raced into Casey's arms.

He staggered back a step, but caught me. "You're okay, thank God."

I held tight, my face buried in his shoulder as I lost control. The tears tore loose. "Lutz is dead and it's my fault."

"You can explain it all when we get off the range."

I recognized the voice, pulling free of Casey. "Daniel?"

A tall thin man stepped into the headlights. The bright lights created shadows on his hard sculpted cheeks. His eagle eyes reflected the lights, cutting as they stared at me. He was a carbon copy of our father and right now, wearing his hair long and braided. "Mother called us, ordered we to come here together. Our brothers wait at the highway."

Casey nodded. "She was quite explicit that I do nothing without Daniel."

"Get me out of here." I wiped tears off my face as fast as they kept coming out.

"You ride with Casey." Daniel headed for my truck. Casey pulled me back into his arms.

I let him, clinging to his shirt. "I shouldn't have let him come with me."

"You shouldn't have come out here at all." He chastised, but gently. "Come on." He guided me towards the truck, Daniel's truck. Giving me a hand up.

Daniel stepped in, putting my backpack on the floor and handing me the Sig. I slipped it back into my holster.

"You got a gun?"

"Am I breathing?" Daniel walked away.

Casey watched him for a moment, tense, then he looked at me. "We really have to talk." He turned the truck around and in seconds the desert rushed past us. I closed my eyes.

I was with Casey and Daniel. I was safe. The terror faded away.

I sat on the rocks beside Lutz' body. I'd straightened his broken limbs and now he faced the sky. I sang the song my mother sang at funerals, brushing his body with branches of sage. Only this wasn't some vague acquaintance. He was my responsibility. He was my friend. It was hard to get the words out with the tears.

"This is not your fault." The image of Lutz appeared and sat down on the other side of the body. The coyotes joined him, nuzzling his cheeks as he stroked their backs. "I

wouldn't let you come out here alone to face that monster and his freak-ass offspring."

"What..." He nodded as I started to ask how he knew about that creature.

"I have been with you since my physical death." He looked to his body, to the coyotes. "My vessel is protected until you return."

"I'm going to."

"Good." Lutz gave me a grin. "So, how do we kill this evil Maxa'xak and his perverted babies?"

"What do you mean 'we'?" I fluttered a hand at his apparition.

"Well, I might not have a real body, but I'm sure there's something I can contribute." His grin drooped. "I'll be around until the final thread holding me here is severed. Something you'll have to do."

"Because I got you killed?" I couldn't look at him or his body. "Maybe if I'd known more about what was out here, I wouldn't have come out here at all. I'd have waited for my brothers, for Casey, for... a few squads of killer Marines."

"Sure, the Marines are all into hunting a giant snake. The second we reported that, we'd have been arrested for smoking peyote."

I laughed. "You don't smoke peyote."

His Spirit shrugged. "Maybe you should give it a try when you get home so I can live vicariously through you."

"Not funny."

He shrugged. "One's sense of humor changes on this side." He petted the big coyote, probably the pack leader. "You want revenge. I can feel it simmering in your body. Remember your training, spiritual and military. If you let revenge drive you, you will make mistakes. Honor me, by doing what you were born to do. With a single focus, hunt down this monster and kill it." Lutz stood up. "Then you can release me, friend."

He faded away, but I could still feel him. His energy remained, attached to me. I set the cleansing sage on his chest. As he asked, the ritual would have to wait. I let my eyes drift up the face of the cliff.

It would wait until I avenged his death.

I tried to stand up, but realized I wasn't sitting in the desert over Lutz' body. I was in a bed. Not my bed. I sat up to get my bearings. The room wasn't dark, but no lights were on. It took a second to realize it was me. I was glowing like I had after my first dream. Like I did in the desert.

It wasn't a surprise this time, but the faces staring at me from the side of the bed were. "Daniel, Joey, Frankie, Chucky." Between them was Casey and he looked three notches past freaked out. "Casey."

"Din'ah." My brothers said in unison. Daniel had a smirk on his face. He and Frankie were standing just a tad behind Casey, somewhat blocking him in.

I looked down at my arms. "I can explain." I tried to brush the glow away, but it didn't let up. "Well, no I can't. Daniel, how do I make it stop?"

"You're asking the wrong person. We don't glow in the dark. Just the females do." He snickered. "The Rising will teach you to control this." He grabbed Joey by the collar. "Let's leave. Lucy got some 'splainin' to do to Ricky."

His Spanish accent was exaggerated from some old, old 1950s TV series. He started teasing Casey when he learned his real name was Ricardo, though I was certainly no wacky redhead.

Joey grinned. "I'm sure our future brother-in-law's got a lot of questions."

"I'm sure he does." Over their teasing protests, Daniel cleared the room.

CHAPTER 16

A hotel room. "Where are we?"

"Outskirts of town." Casey moved around to the foot of the bed. "Ahhhh, how long does this last?"

"I don't know. I didn't know anything about this until it happened…" I looked at the clock next to the bed. "…yesterday morning."

"Okay. Does it… hurt?"

"No. It's a bit warm." I swung my legs off the bed and stood up. "Maybe a shower will make it go away. I need one anyway."

"Shower. Joey got us some clothes. Then we talk."

My backpack was on the chair next to the bed. I fished around and found the camera, handing it to Casey. "I will, but look at the evidence. It's all in here, or most of it. They're linked to that truckload of bodies, but I didn't get that recorded." I circled around him to get to the bathroom, trying not to touch him. "I'm sorry you had to find out about… whatever this is, this way. Just give me a few minutes. Please."

"Din'ah!" He called me by my real name as I turned away.

"I know, this isn't what you expected. I'll understand if you can't… do this."

He grabbed my arm and swung me back to face him. "Are you expecting me to run?"

I couldn't look at him, not after seeing his expression when I woke up.

"Din'ah. I'm not going anywhere." He pulled me into his arms, holding me.

I shivered, despite the heat inside my body. "I don't know what's going to happen, but it's going to be bad. I don't want to lose you, too."

"You won't." He caught my face and forced me to look up at him. "I promise." He gave me a kiss, a deep kiss. The kind of kiss that sent a flutter out from my insides, spreading down to make my knees weak. He picked that moment to let go, giving me a wicked little grin. "Go get your shower."

I headed to the little bathroom. Real little. There wasn't room for a tub, but I didn't need one. I stripped off my BDU pants, the pant leg ripped and bloody. Wait… I'd been wounded. My clothes proved it, but all there was on my leg was dried blood and a raw strip of reddened flesh, instead of an open wound.

I poked at it. It stung, almost as bad as an open wound might. But it wasn't open anymore.

Where I poked, my flesh glowed brighter. Was aggravating the wound sending more energy to the area? "Okay. I guess that's a benefit."

I stepped into a cold shower and turned it to scalding, but lukewarm was the best I got. It took a while, with the irregular sprinkling of water, to wash the sweat and dirt off. Just as I was getting ready to reach out for the cheap hotel shampoo, Casey shoved my favorite brand through the curtain, along with my conditioner.

Silently I thanked Joey for thinking to grab them.

With the trickling water it took twice as long to get my hair washed, about as long as it took to chill me to the bone. The glow was gone when I opened my eyes. I was human again as I stepped out of the shower and wrapped myself in the only towels they provided. Barely dish towels. I reminded myself… cheap hotel.

In the mirror I could see my eyes were puffy. I'd cried when Casey found me and in my dream as Lutz tried to comfort me. *I never cry*. Between my brothers and the Marines, I'd learned not to cry, no matter how bad things got. But I'd passed 'no matter how bad' by miles, so I didn't chide myself for letting go.

Stepping out of the bathroom, Casey was on the phone. "Yes, sir. I appreciate this. With this current case I can't be there for a day or two." A moment of silence. "Yeah, her partner will enjoy it and maybe learn a little more about the locals. Never hurts, right?" He nodded, holding a finger to his lips when he saw me. "Great. Thank you." He hung up.

"Who were you talking to?"

"Your CO. You and Lutz are officially off duty for the next week in observance of a religious ceremony you've been ordered to attend." He removed his utility belt and ripped open the Velcro straps of his boots, kicking them off.

"Really? Where'd you come up with that story?"

"Daniel."

"You called my commander, at this hour?"

"No, I called the duty officer, who just happened to be the CO taking the shift."

"You told him Lutz was going to a religious ceremony with me. He's dead. That's hard to fake, you know."

"We need time and refusing you religious time off is discriminatory." Casey stripped off his shirt and Kevlar, hanging them over the back of a chair. "He didn't ask anything more than how many days you needed."

"Seriously, out of the blue I start claiming religious privileges?"

"I told them there was some upheaval in the Nation and because of your family's ranking, your presence was demanded. Something to do with the NCT-whatever. When you start throwing religion and as string of government agencies around, people prefer to cooperate then get drawn into it."

He went to the table, sorting through several grocery bags. "You need to eat something. Frank went to the quick mart down on the corner."

Hunger hadn't even vaguely crossed my mind. I looked over the array. A couple microwave burritos, a reasonably fresh looking ham sandwich, a hoagie, cheese sticks, bags of chips, sodas and a handful of mixed condiments. A mini-buffet of junk food. I took the sandwich, chips and a soda, then crawled onto the bed.

"Really!" Casey rolled his eyes at me, taking the hoagie and grabbing a handful of the packets. "We have a table."

"If I sit down I might not get up again."

"I'd have taken care of that." He moved my backpack off the arm chair and sat down, dropping the packets on the nightstand. "You look better. Your leg is… healing."

"Yeah, go figure." I poked it gently, getting nothing of the glow this time. I turned my arm a bit as I reached for mustard. "Back to normal, I guess. I think it happens when I get emotional. Twice it was in dreams."

"And the other times?"

"When I saw Lutz at the bottom…" I took a breath, making sure I didn't lose it again. "…at the bottom of the cliff. I was upset and scared, and angry. Then the coyotes started to show up. They protected him."

I shook my head as those minutes replayed in my head. "It wasn't just the coyotes. It sounds crazy to say it out loud, but the animal Spirits came out to protect me too. I had to crawl into a hole to hide, only to find out it was a nest full of rattlers. They left me alone, but threatened the men. Then the coyotes..."

Using the food as a moment to remember it all, I took a bite of my sandwich, holding a finger up as I chewed. A few chips made it taste better. Another bite and drink. "I didn't glow with the snakes. Not until the coyotes came out. I was afraid they'd attack him and that's when it happened. They all laid down around him and started to… to sing."

I choked up again. "Not howling. It was so mournful. The pack leader was looking right at me and I was glowing again. He was telling me they'd protect him until I returned. Then another pack showed up to lead me down the mountain. When the enemy helicopter came looking for me, they used their bodies to hide me."

Casey was squinting.

"I know it sounds insane, but that's what happened."

He rolled his eyes away from me. "If I hadn't seen you light up like a nuclear reactor, I'd be checking you into the loony bin."

"Did you look at the video?" I looked around and saw the camera next to the phones. "That's crazy. It's monsters and zombies right out of some damned D-rated movie."

"I haven't watched it yet. It will wait until we download it and show it to everyone."

He lingered through a bite of his sandwich, still not looking at me.

"Is something wrong? Other than everything?"

"No..." He wrapped up what was left of his sandwich and put it on the nightstand. He leaned forward, his elbows propped on his knees, looking at his hands. "Except for something your brothers said."

"They were teasing. You know they only do that because they like you."

"Not that. About us." Closing my eyes I replayed those few minutes. It hit me. He lifted his eyes to meet mine. "Is it even possible now for us to have a future together?"

"Oh, Casey…" I crawled across the bed, going to him. His arms wrapped around me as I climbed onto his lap. "It has to be."

CHAPTER

17

His arms held me tight, his face pressed against my neck. "Whatever's happening, I don't want to lose you."

I combed my fingers through his hair. "You won't. And when this is done…" I pulled my shoulders back enough to look up at him. His dark brown eyes were so clear, so open, pulling me into them. "…I'm going to marry you."

His hands caught my face. "I already knew it. The first day you came marching up to my truck, I said, 'that's her. I'm going to marry her'. Nothing's going to stop me. Not even some freaky monster out to destroy the world." He pulled my face to his, kissing me as his arms grabbed me up. I clung to his neck as he took the two steps to the bed. He lowered me down, still kissing me as he knelt over me. I tugged at his t-shirt as he got his pants off.

My heart thudded as his body crushed down on mine. The passion of the night before was nothing compared to the look in his eyes now. I clutched at the sheets as he pushed deep inside me, all at once. I let out a cry and he thrust deeper. My whole body rose to meet his and he groaned as my insides tightened around him, but he didn't stop. Not even as an orgasm tore through me.

He leaned over me, shifting our bodies, but only so he could kiss me. His hands released my hips, not that it mattered with my legs clamped around him. His fingers untangled mine from the sheets, intertwining them with his.

Our mouths muffled the groans from both of us. When he finally reached his own orgasm, I'd had at least three. He rested on his elbows, our bodies still one as he brushed a strand of hair from my face. "You're glowing."

I laughed. "Thanks."

"No, babe, you're glowing again." He reached up over the bed and turned off the light.

The room went dark, except around me. "Oh, great." Breathing was still too raspy to say anything more.

"Well, you're not dreaming and no one's threatening you, so I'm glad to see good emotions inspire this look too." He smirked.

"Guess so." I managed a smile and a little squirm of my hips.

"Stop!" He pinned me down again. He kissed my neck right below my ear. "You go moving around and I won't be able to help myself."

"Not a persuasive argument."

Casey's fingers stroked my cheek. "I shouldn't have been so rough. I was… possessed." His lips returned to that spot on my neck. "You're finally mine, heart and soul."

"And Spirit, apparently."

We clung to each other until our bodies were calm again, only shifting around to let me breathe. Casey ran his fingers along my leg where I had it laced with his. "You're almost faded out again."

"When this is over, you can light me up all you want." I nestled my head into his shoulder. "I'm tired… and tomorrow…"

"Tomorrow we have to figure out what to do next." He pulled the blanket over us, keeping me in his arms.

I wanted to sleep, but apprehension crept in over the ecstasy. Casey covered my absence. My family would all be here. Lutz gave me his blessing to avenge him. So we were going to hunt down this Maxa'xak. It was our duty, an obligation passed down through the generations. What if we failed? What if we won? What would happen to us?

Maybe Casey had a reason to be afraid. I had serious doubts things would magically return to normal.

The questions kept me from real sleep, only achieving an odd numbness as I drifted on that edge. Not asleep enough to miss the light on the phone as it flickered an advance warning of an incoming call. I nudged Casey as it started to actually ring.

He answered it, sounding as groggy as I felt. "Yeah." A string of monosyllable responses followed before he hung up. "We're going to have visitors." He swung his legs out of bed, pulling on his pants and t-shirt. "So much for you getting some sleep."

"Let me straighten up a bit." I crawled out of bed, heading to the bathroom. I'd gone to bed with damp hair and it was tossed and tangled now. I managed to comb it out, braid and tie it off. Casey brought me shorts and a t-shirt, my less than romantic sleepwear.

Someone knocked. Casey peeked out the window, then opened the door. Daniel came in, followed by four more people. I only knew one of them. "Yazzie?"

She stood among the group of Cocopah. "Capt. Castle." She bowed her head. "We are here to do the bidding of the Star People."

I looked to Daniel. "They will retrieve your friend. Then take him to their village until this is over."

"I can't… we can't send other people up there."

"It is better we do this, so the evil Spirit will not know you still exist." Yazzie stepped forward. "We have valid reasons to be in the mountains, and the means."

"They have a helicopter." Daniel nodded to Casey.

"And we have range clearance to retrieve plants necessary for our… rituals." Yazzie pointed to other men in her group. "We do it all the time, so the enemy will not suspect us."

"They'll suspect a missing body."

Casey shrugged. "It could be played in our favor. The sooner they get there, the less likely they'll discover there aren't two bodies."

"We can make it look like we retrieved two." Yazzie confidently raised her chin.

"I don't know…"

"It is necessary. His Spirit is still connected to his body and his body is vulnerable."

Daniel stepped closer, gazing down at me. "It will give us time and putting your friend into cool storage will mislead investigators on the time of his death."

We couldn't leave him out there. Decomp would be rapid once the sun came up and Casey had just reported him as alive and well with the tribe. I had no choice but to agree. Their pilot pulled up a map and I point out the cliffs. He knew the spot and could get the helicopter in close enough. Flying low, the enemy might not even know they were there, until it was too late.

The plan in place, Yazzie assured me again that they knew what they were doing. I told her of the coyotes and to take them a bag of jerky. I got some strange looks from the men, but Yazzie gave me a nod, urging them to leave.

CHAPTER 18

Daniel remained. “You need to gather up your stuff. We’re moving.”

“Where?” I took a step backwards. “Shouldn’t I be keeping a low profile?”

“Relax. We’re not going to the mountains.” Daniel glared at me. “Did you get any sleep?” He didn’t need an answer. Casey was blushing vividly. “We need someplace we can gather without drawing attention.”

“And where’s that? We don’t know how far their reach is. They had someone on base.”

“Maybe, but they can’t be everywhere.” Casey picked up his uniform shirt. “When do we move and to where? I need to swing by the office and check in.”

“You’re going to work?” I clamped my lips together when I heard my voice come out panicked. Definitely not portraying the tough Marine right now.

“I can’t just disappear.” He started buttoning up his shirt. “I’ll go in and set it up with my second to hand the reins over to him. Then I’ll catch up with you. Wherever that is.”

“If they were watching you, then they know you came out into the desert last night to get me. They might have followed us here. Probably have a tracker on your truck.”

Casey gave me a smile I knew well, his patient ‘got it covered, babe’ smile when I was trying to tell him something he already knew. “I dropped my regular truck off at the shop before going on that call yesterday. When I realized you were missing I pulled a random UC truck from the lot to come looking for you.”

“Charles will follow you in and bring you back to us when you’re all clear.” Daniel moved over to the door. “The Cocopah put one of their casino hotels at our disposal. We can hide in plain sight. No one’s going to notice a few dozen more Indians on the reservation.”

“A few dozen? Last count there’s only seven in the family, Casey makes eight. That doesn’t exactly scream invasion forces.”

Daniel closed his eyes, shaking his head. “Just a babe in the woods, aren’t you, Din’ah.” He looked at me again with that impatience he had when I was a kid. “We are an old people, spread out over the many states. All of us diligently watching for signs and you just blindly stumbled on our prey.”

“Doing my job, on patrol, so there was no ‘stumbling’ involved.” I snapped at him, resenting the stupid kid treatment. “And how would I know anything about all this? I’ve been kept in the dark, always told ‘when the time comes’. If I’d had a clue, maybe I wouldn’t have gone back up there to try to figure things out. Maybe my friend might still…" The rage ignited the thing inside me, burning up through my flesh. I jerked my arms out. "STOP IT!"

I ran to the bath and slammed the door, sliding down the back of it. If I'd known, something, anything, Lutz might be out there helping us plot how to get to these guys. Or he'd be safely on base stuck on desk duty until this was over. And now Casey was involved too. I just promised him forever, but we had to go into some kind of battle with some weird-assed dark Spirit that had been around for thousands of years.

My head ached with all the ugly images. That monster, those innocent illegals, Lutz' twisted and broken body, even some of the nightmares left over from the Middle East. If myths were true, what was the Great Father's or Mother's plan to forever burden the Star People with the task of hunting Maxa'xak? How did I end up in the center of this? *Why me?*

I ignored the rapping on the door. "Beth? Come out. Your brother is gone." He knocked again, then stopped, though I could feel him on the other side of the door. He waited a couple minutes, then I heard him again. Through the cheap fiberboard separating us, his voice came through as if his lips were whispering in my ear. "I'd freak out too. It's a lot for any sane person to deal with. No one can blame you for wanting to run away, but I know you. You don't run. We're not runners."

I turned my head against the door. "What am I? If all this is real, than I'm not any more human than that monster is. You didn't look at the video. You didn't see it. If that's what it looks like, what will I turn into?"

"I have to assume something still human. Look at your mother. Aside from some strange…" He didn't finish the sentence. She'd embarrassed him often enough to and keep him on his toes around her. "Listen, babe, you won't know more until you ask her. We're going to the hotel. You'll get a little more rest, then we'll figure all this out."

"You've got to go into the office." I turned more, putting my hand to the door where he was crouched on the other side. "I'm… scared. What if they figured out you tricked them? What if they have someone in your offices too?"

"I think they'd have hit us here if they had. This isn't exactly Fort Knox." He laughed softly, but under it was a tone of seriousness. "Listen, if you're that worried I'll see if Daniel can change up the plan a bit. We'll go to my office together. You can stay in the back office with Charles while I set everything up."

I didn't respond and he didn't push me. My skin stung a bit from the intensity of this episode, but I was transitioning back to normal. I needed to get a grip on this fear and this weird thing inside me. Another deep breath and I let out a sigh. "No. Go. I'll meet you at the hotel."

"Okay, but not until I can see you're all right." His voice had shifted. He was standing up. I turned the lock on the door as I got off the floor, opening it. He immediately pulled me into an embrace. "I promise I won't be long. Just stick to Daniel's side until he has you to safety."

"I will." I gave him another hug. "I need a few minutes to get ready, so go."

Casey gave me a kiss and another hug, then pulled on a civilian windbreaker, adding a cowboy hat. It was still dark enough no one would notice the uniform underneath. Chucky was waiting outside.

Frankie was there too. "I got the room covered. Get yourself ready to move."

I locked the door and took another shower. A quick one, but the cold water totally woke up my nerves. I dressed in the civvies Joey had for packed. I half-expected him to pull out the ugliest of everything I had, but he'd packed for hunting. Nothing to draw attention. Jeans, dark t-shirt, boots, my cowboy hat.

I shoved my dirty clothes into the duffle as I heard a rapping on the door. It was Daniel. He didn't say anything as I let him in. He just gathered up our stuff. Frankie wrapped an arm over my shoulder as he walked me down the stairs to their truck. "How you doing, Sis?"

"Tired, confused, scared."

"If you weren't, I'd be worried."

He kept his arm around me, a ball cap dangling from his hand. I realized it was intentional, raised just enough to cover the rest of my face. He kept me on the inside railing, using his body to block anyone watching street-side. Daniel added another layer of coverage for the few steps it took to reach the truck.

They put me in the back passenger seat. The windows were dark tinted, but also had pull down screens to further block out the sun. They were down already, even though the sun was just creeping over the horizon.

As we headed for the highway, I saw Joey pull out of the convenience market across the street, driving Billy's truck. He fell in behind us. Not so close as to be obvious, but close enough we could keep an eye on each other.

Daniel looked at me in the rear view mirror. "Ricky will join us on the Res."

"I'm pretty sure you know he hates being called that."

"I'm pretty sure you know I won't stop." He winked at me, then shrugged. "However, in mixed company we'll give Officer Delgado the respect he deserves. That work for you?"

"I'm sure it will."

Frankie turned around in his seat to face me. "He's a good man. We've never had anything but respect for him. We knew from the first day he was a keeper. It's not easy to find that one person our inner Spirit can bond with."

"A pure Spirit." I shook my head, looking out the little crack between window and shade. Maybe if I'd known a bit more about…us, I could've saved a lot of late night fights."

"Yeah, you'd have believed us. Hey, Sis, we're aliens tasked with the job of chasing down other alien monsters, and killing them."

I jerked my head around to look at him. "Who said anything about us being aliens?" Out came the denial he'd just used as their excuse for not telling the truth.

Frankie stared back at me, unblinking. "Gods, spirits, ghosts, demons… we all grew up with TV shows espousing they were aliens. Guess what, in this case we are. Primitive humans needed to explain what they saw in the simplest ways possible. Earth's people are humans, everything else isn't. That includes us."

He didn't blink and glancing at Daniel, he didn't look at me. So much for someone telling me we weren't aliens. I wanted so much to hear those words.

Frankie laughed at my silent attempt to cling to hope. "You'll see. When mother brings you the rest of the way over."

Daniel shot Frankie a glare and he turned around. Daniel's eyes met mine for a second, then back to the road ahead. "You know all this. Your Star Spirit is waking up. You just don't know how to integrate yet. You will by the end of the day."

He was using his leader of the pack voice, flat, firm and inviting no questions or dissent.

CHAPTER

19

I turned back to the window, watching as he got on the highway heading west. I knew where the new casino was. I'd grown up hearing my parents discussing Nation politics, teaching it to us. After being shattered by the spread of the white man across this continent, the People finally reunited in this century, as a true Nation.

All the People were now one People. As one People they entered into court battles against the U.S. Government to regain their most historic homelands. Unity and determination yielded rulings all over the country, even involving Canada and Mexico.

For the Cocopah, they won back their traditional river lands grabbed by the U.S. Government and Mexico over the previous two hundred years. The revised Cocopah territory carved out four hundred square miles, mostly between Arizona and Mexico, spanning both sides of the Colorado River.

There was an immediate panic as Imminent Domain was established. But the Cocopah worked to quickly quell the unrest. One-hundred year land grants were issued to many of the current non-tribal home and business owners who wanted to remain inside the new territory.

There were no grants offered for the lands immediately around the Colorado River itself. That long swath of river land was declared sacred Cocopah land. The tribe removed all offensive buildings, cleaned up the wetlands and rebuilt recreational areas.

Lands too damaged to be returned to wild lands were used to build new hotels, restaurants and shiny casinos all interconnected along the river, creating a Cocopah Riviera. Eco-friendly tourism brought in revenue for new schools, hospitals and community programs.

The tribe balanced the new with the old. Every Cocopah spoke their native language and observed tribal traditions, but also spoke English and excelled in U.S. standardized education. The younger generations were effectively encouraged to be competitive with the rest of the United States, and the world.

In less than a decade, Arizona had a Cocopah woman in the U.S. Senate. One elected mostly by the non-tribal population. Their successes and failures set example to all the other tribes in the Nation. Restoring harmony to the People. A harmony my parents talked about with personal great pride, at the same time keeping the truth of my heritage a secret.

A pothole jarred my thoughts away from the past. Ironically we were headed south on 95. We passed signs warning people they were entering the reservation and subject to tribal laws. Nothing other than the signs really changed, except that being the last pothole we were likely to hit. Arizona wasn't as progressive as the Nation on their side of the 95.

The tribal side of the highway was a wide new expanse, still patrolled by DPS. An interagency agreement made sure criminals couldn't just jump the territorial line to avoid pursuit. Suspects caught on tribal lands they were handed over immediately. Their tough policy was an effective dissuasion and cut down the costs of supporting non-tribal prisoners.

We passed the 'Last Chance' sign and were on the Cocopah Reservation.

Even though I had a lot of Cocopah friends, and I liked it on the Res, I didn't come this way often. Other than concerts or events, my visits were usually representing the USMC. Typically, as their token 'Indian', I got tapped as liaison if one of our boys got into trouble. It didn't happen often. Newbies were briefed that the last person they ever wanted coming after them, was me. I could make a Marine cry, and would.

Leaning my face against the window, I watched the buildings go by. Right now I wasn't coming onto the Res as a friend, rock fan or Marine, but as a refugee. I suddenly felt... different... displaced. Unsure if I'd ever fit into any of these worlds again.

In the distance I saw a long swath of green. The Colorado River. It wasn't far now. The new casino was close to San Luis. I'd be there soon and could sleep, maybe get rid of this feeling of... dread. No, not dread. I felt something else. Something overwhelming the weariness of a sleepless night. Jittery, as if... pursued.

I looked behind us and saw Joey about three cars behind us. He was looking around him, looking as jittery as I felt. My skin got warmer. “Daniel! Something’s wrong.”

Right then Frankie’s phone chirped. He flipped it to the dash speaker. “What’s up?”

“Someone’s behind me. A big tan SUV.” I could see Joey talking as he tailed us. “I’ve changed lanes but they’re not passing. I’m getting off at the next exit.” Joey was the youngest of my brothers, but still older than me. He’d been put through the same brotherly torture I had, so I was closer to him. My heart thudded as he took the off ramp. The SUV followed him. “Still on my bumper.”

“I know this exit!” I threw myself against the seatbelt, shouting over Frankie’s shoulder. “Take a left at the light and about a half mile on the right is the police maintenance yard. Billy… the guy who owns that truck, he’s tribal police. Officer William Ortiz.”

“Do as she says. Stay there until Charles comes to pick you up.”

“Got it… turning left… still behind me. Two guys. I can see a rental tag in the window.”

“You should be able to see the sign, and a lot of outside light posts. There’s a guard at the gate. He’ll run the plate when you pull in and probably open the gate without stopping you.”

“Pulling in and… there goes the gate.” There was a laugh. “Ha! They don’t look too pleased to see where I led them. They just tore out of here. They’re gone.”

“Don’t count on it.” Daniel changed to the exit lane to get us off the highway too. “They’ll turn around and watch the place. Get out so they can see you're not Din'ah or Casey. That'll confuse them."

"And alert the guards. Tell them to call Billy… William Ortiz. Tell him you're my brother and…" And what? I was supposed to return the truck and bikes yesterday.

Daniel looked at me in the mirror, that stern 'I'm in charge here' look. "Let them get a glimpse of you, nothing more. Then get inside to do any explaining." His eyes flipped to his own rearview mirrors, looking to see if anyone followed us off the highway.

Joey kept his phone active, picking up the conversation with the duty officers on the gate. Giving us a blow-by-blow as they called Billy. Joey found a front window. "The SUV swung into the McDonalds across the street, facing the maintenance yard. They're still inside, fighting from appearances."

Daniel switched to city streets, making several more turns, slowing down to see who turned next, speeding up to put lights between us and other vehicles.

I called Chucky. "They followed Joey. I sent him to the Santa Fe District Police Yard. Casey knows where it is. Pick him up and have Casey call Billy. Make something up and tell him we'll… that we needed to hang onto the bikes, something believable." He'd be sorry to lose them, but he didn't need to know until this was over.

Daniel added a few more instructions, sounding a bit peeved and tossing me a glare. I shut down my phone.

The jitters let go as we zigzagged through town, the dread diminished to match. I eased back into the corner. "So, I know I'm supposed to wait, but what just happened? Was my Star Spirit trying to warn me something was wrong?"

"You're getting stronger. You felt it nearly as fast as Joey did." Daniel didn't snip at me, instead sounding a bit impressed. "Your run in with these guys must have been pretty intense, to have triggered such a rapid Rising."

"It was." I hunkered down a bit more in the back seat. "If I can feel them, can they feel me? Is that why they were following us? Do you think they know I'm not dead?"

"They didn't touch you, did they?" Daniel's eyes were on me again.

"NO! I never took my gun off the pack leader until I drove away. He got close, maybe four feet from me. It took everything not to shoot him." I shivered, remembering that moment. "He was… creepy. Beady-eyed, but not a hint of emotions. Just an ugly smirk."

I got head nods. "He couldn't know what you are unless he actually touched you." He did a mirror check as we took another corner. "They must have latched onto the truck when we sent Joey to your apartment. As good as he is getting in and out of places, they're just as good at hiding in the cracks."

Frankie shrugged. "Hopefully we've confused them."

"Hope so."

"He'll do a recon before Charles gets there."

"There's a back gate to the complex." I pulled out my phone, sending Chucky a text.

"Hey, enough with the calls!" Frankie reached back for my phone.

I evaded him. "I'm not an idiot. We switched to burners. And the message is vague. To anyone watching it'll look like a drug hookup. I did learn a little counter-intelligence in the Marines."

"Which explains a lot. That being counter of real intelligence." Frankie sniped at me.

"Shut up, Francis!" He hated that name.

"Knock it off!" Daniel was louder than both of us. "We weren't thrilled when you joined the Marines, but it was probably the best thing. Your training gave you skills we could only gloss over until you came into your own."

He gave me a softer glance. "It just drove us a bit crazy that we couldn't keep you safe anymore."

"Oh, is that what you called it when we were growing up?"

Frankie didn't say anything, staring out the window. From the tension in his jaw, I knew he was struggling to not argue. I'd fought with my brothers a lot growing up, but it was the usual sibling stuff. When I announced I was going into the Marines, he freaked out the most. Since then there was a strange distance between us. Now probably wasn't the time to keep feeding it.

Instead I started keying in access to my virtual laptop. I had to erase the automated messages Lutz and I left. The sound of the phone keys made Frankie jerk around again. "I need to delete the 'come look for us' message I programmed for auto-delivery." He scowled. So much for not antagonizing him. I wiped my call history, removed the battery and internal cards, then rolled down the window and tossed the phone out into the street. "All done."

Frankie gave me a nod and I went back to watching the road behind us.

CHAPTER 20

I saw the casino. It had opened just the week before. Special promotions and A-List headliners were drawing in crowds of people. "Is this what you consider hiding? Every media group is here this week for the grand opening."

Neither answered me as we went around to the back of the complex and were let through a private entrance, being directed to the rear pavilion. Usually the back of a complex was industrial, but this entrance faced the river and was as luxurious as the main facade, just smaller.

Two security guards met us as we pulled into the circular drive. Frankie opened my door to let me out and they immediately surrounded me. I was buried in broad shoulders as they escorted me into the hotel's foyer.

My brothers replaced them as they returned to the truck to get our bags.

I had a minute or less to take a look around the foyer. It was clearly set up to cater to celebrities or private guests who didn't want to advertise their presence, but expected the best of everything.

Glittering quartz granites caught and reflected light around the lobby, bouncing off polished dark rich woods. A chandelier hung low and sparkled. Though the metal and gems glimmered, the design looked ancient. It was. Their eco-policy required as much recycled materials as possible, so they used a lot of antiques in their hotels.

Starring up at the chandelier, I caught a flicker in the corner of my eye. The gorgeous wood wall opened and an immaculately groomed woman in a tailored black suit stepped out. She approached me, not the least bit fazed by my Levis and t-shirt.

"Ms. Adams. It is my honor to meet you. I am Cherise Begay, your personal concierge. Anything you require will be provided with the upmost of discretion." She nodded towards the two security guards behind us.

I didn't attempt to correct my name. It didn't take a Bond genius to know we wouldn't be using real names. "Thank you, Cherise."

She gave me a slight smile. "The members of your convention have already been accommodated. The penthouse floors are available to your party, exclusively. All service individuals have been vetted by your own people, but if you have any concerns, alert the security immediately." She stepped aside. "If you'll accompany me, I'll take you to your suites."

I looked at the two guards behind us, looking grim and ready to react if necessary. I met eyes with Daniel, but he didn't flinch. I turned back to the woman. "Lead the way."

She crossed to the wall she'd exited and with a wave of her hand it opened to reveal an elevator. It wasn't a small elevator, apparently intended for 'entourages'. With the six of us and luggage, there was still room left over. There were only a few buttons on the panel. Ground floor, concierge level, four penthouse levels and a roof lounge.

She pulled a small tablet from inside her jacket and slid a black key card over the scanner eye, handing it to me. The second my fingertips touched the card, her screen flashed an acknowledgment. "This is your access card, keyed to your fingerprints alone. If you lose it, it is of no value to anyone who finds it. If you would insert it here."

It was an impressive security measure. The black card had nothing on it. Not even the hotel's name. I followed her instructions and the elevator started up. "You and your immediate entourage have access to all floors serviced by this elevator. The concierge level will give you access to the main casino. The other members of your convention will have access to all penthouse levels, except yours. That is exclusive to your immediate entourage."

My convention? Entourage? Four penthouse floors? Daniel said no one would notice "a few dozen" more of us. If we needed four floors, that qualified as a convention. I wanted to ask Daniel what was going on. Instead I kept my mouth shut. Ms. Begay seemed to think I was the leader of this group, instead of the village idiot.

The elevator ride up lasted only a few seconds, bypassing PH4, PH3, PH2, stopping at PH1. "Here we are." She extended her hand with a head bow, inviting me to exit first.

I obliged, stepping out into a glass hallway wide enough to entertain a large reception or party. Possibly used for exactly that purpose with the layout of elegant tables, chairs, sofas and a full-service bar. The floor-to-ceiling glass wall faced east, towards the mountains. If not for knowing what those mountains protected, for what Yazzie and her crew were doing this instant, recovering Lutz' body, they might have made for a breathtaking view.

But I knew the truth.

Cherise cleared her throat, drawing my attention away from the view. There were more security guards, large, broad-chested, clean shaven and dressed impeccably. They stood at either side of the elevator. "Mr. and Mrs. Adams are at the end of the corridor."

Mrs. Adams... oh yeah, my mother.

She didn't seem to notice the second of confusion. "The rooms between are assigned to the Adams brothers." She bowed her head to Daniel, but urged me down the long corridor in the opposite direction of my mother's room. "And these are your rooms."

She stepped ahead of me to open a set of double doors, stepping into the apartment and waving her hand like a game-show model. "I hope this meets your needs."

Two steps in and I did my best to not drag my chin on the deep carpet. Daniel gave me a little nudge to snap me out of my moment of brain fog "Thank you, Cherise. This looks… lovely."

She smiled with that hint of smugness that said she knew they were the best accommodations to be found, on par with the best in the world. Not conceit, but certainty. She waved to the security guards with our luggage. Frankie was quick to intervene, stopping them and pointing out my and Casey's bags.

He took them from the guard. Daniel gave me an eye flick, that silent language we had as kids that said to get rid of the outsiders. Cherise had already started to point out the room's amenities. I stepped up and put my hand on her arm. "I'm sorry. I'm exhausted. I think I'll show myself the suite, if you don't mind."

"Oh, certainly!" She smiled at me warmly. "If you have any needs or questions, I am at your 24-hour disposal." She turned to Daniel. "I will await you by the elevators and get your keys set up."

He bowed to her, giving one of his charming smiles we saw so seldom, as he walked her and the guards to the doors. "We'll only be a moment."

He closed the doors on her and Frankie carried our bags to the bedroom. I followed him and was as stunned by the opulence of this room as I was with the sitting room. "Who the hell is paying for this? Let alone four floors of suites."

"That's not your concern." He swung our bags up on the luggage shelf next to the dresser.

"Actually, it is." Daniel joined us. "The Cocopah will bill the Council."

"The National Council, as in Tribal Affairs, in DC?"

"The one and only." He went to the wall of curtains and pulled them back. "Wow, spectacular view."

"Seriously, Daniel." I stomped up beside him, trying to ignore the dizzying twenty story drop straight down the back face of the hotel. I could see gardens below and the river. There was a dock with a paddleboat moored down, allowing tourists to board. I pulled myself away from the view. "What does the NCTA have to do with this?"

"Everything." Daniel leaned against the window, making me nervous, though I was sure the hotel had installed glass thick enough to be nearly bullet-proof, if it wasn't. "Long story into the short, our tribe is scattered throughout the Nation, assimilating into areas where the Maxa'xak might have fled. We constantly track events the local police can't explain. Or things most people write off as drugs or alcohol. Strange sightings of large snakes in the rivers, ghost men, unexplained, gruesome deaths..."

"Shit like that happens all the time."

"Increases in unsolved missing persons." Daniel raised an eyebrow at me. "Whole family groups have disappeared. The Yahi. Now illegals. The Maxa'xak found a perfect source of bodies to infest."

"Mom said we failed the Yahi, but that's not what I read in the history records."

"The real story was suppressed. No one, particularly the white men, were going to believe that an evil Spirit grabbed adult males and killed everyone else. They were a lot more willing to believe their own were responsible for the murders. Our people tried to kill the Maxa'xak, but it got away with a few of its children, and we've been tracking it since."

"And the NCTA knows this."

"The NCTA is the Nation." Daniel leaned closer. "It's nearly impossible to keep this big a secret, unless you believe. Ten thousand years they have kept us secret, because they believe. They know we're here to kill this monster, or it will destroy more than the People."

Frankie came into the room. I hadn't seen him leave, but he carried a steaming cup. An odd smell rolled up into my face as he handed it to me. "Mom says you're to drink this and get some real sleep."

I took the cup. It wasn't tea, though it had the right color. It had flecks in it I remembered. She always made us bark teas when we were sick. "I should talk to her first."

"She's not available."

"Really? Do I have to go knocking on her door?"

"No, but she is in one of her meditations." Frankie squinted at me. "Do you really want to try to interrupt that, or just do as she says?"

"No." Whether I needed the tea or not, I drank it down. It was bitter. Way more bitter than I remembered. I shifted to say something to Daniel, but I couldn't remember what. He just nodded in a strange slow motion.

CHAPTER

21

"It's time to wake up, Din'ah."

Hearing my name, I opened my eyes, then struggled up to my elbows. "Lutz?" I looked around. I was in the penthouse suite at the casino. Last I remembered I was talking to Daniel. Then Frankie gave me one of my mother's tea. "Wow, I guess they really wanted me to sleep."

As I went to brush a strand of hair off my face, I saw my hand in front of my face, but also laying on the bed next to my leg, as if I were lying on top of someone. "What the hell?" I tried to roll away, but my body felt stuck, my torso not moving.

"Stop fighting." Lutz reached out and held my shoulder. "Your body is asleep so we can speak to your subconscious, your mortal Spirit. I think it's called Spirit Walking."

I shifted to one side and could see how my being lifted out of the body I was attached to. I felt a lifelessness in my physical body. "You sure I'm not dying, or something?"

"No, dear. You're fine."

I jerked around to see a woman on the other side of the bed. It took a moment to recognize her. "Mom?" She looked so young, so pretty, like pictures of when she was a teenager.

She sat down on the edge of the bed, both Spirits blocking me in. "You grow stronger by the minute." She caressed my face. "You bring me great pride and my deepest fears."

I caught her hand. "I haven't done anything to inspire either."

"You're a decorated soldier who has served this country, in this life and many before, but when you were born I recognized your Spirit. I knew the Great Mother chose you to face the Maxa'xak." She smiled, a sad light in her eyes. "You must allow your Spirit to Rise."

"But..." I looked at my hand again. I wasn't glowing, but I could feel the heat building. "...what happens to me if this Spirit comes out? Where do I go?"

"You will be one person." It sounded simple, but something in her tone told me differently. "Rising brings your inner Spirit into this world. You only know your mortal strengths, but totally awakened, she possesses the ability to draw upon all our Spirits, upon the Spirits of this world. Without these powers, you will be helpless against our enemy."

She squeezed my hand. "You saw that monster. You know you can't fight it as Beth, or as a Marine."

Lutz patted my leg, feeling as real as when he was alive. "You need her. Your people need her."

"So I let her out and..." My heart beat faster, but in this state it felt as if I was feeling someone else's pulse. "...hope I'm still me." It was disconcerting, but oddly familiar. "Okay, so what do I do?"

"Normally the Rising happens slowly, but your Spirit is pressing to come out now. You have to let this happen. Stop fighting her. Trust your Spirit. Trust me." My mother placed her palm to my forehead, pushing me down into the bed, down into my body. She held me there, silently gazing into my eyes. "Surrenders to her." She pressed harder. "Awaken, Din'ah!"

A jolting spark shot through her hand, into my head. My body jerked, but then froze. My vision closed in on itself, turning into my own head. I saw that spark tearing open cells and images flooded out. Strangers, for a split second, before I recognized the Spirits beneath their mortal bodies. Time passed from century to century. Faces changed, but not the Spirits. These were memories. Her memories. The Spirit inside me.

She showed me all her past lives, all the battles, all the deaths, all the rebirths. I saw flashes of my own life, my own experiences, the battle scars I carried on my soul. She had been with me, in a state of conscious hibernation, stirring when I was in danger. Subconscious nudges I took as intuition. But mostly waiting until she was needed.

She had a duty and I could see what was expected of her. I could feel her resolve to fight the Maxa'xak. To free this world of this monster. She had a duty. I just had to let her out. I had to surrender my will to her. I had to surrender.

"Surrender".

I blinked my eyes. It wasn't my mother and Lutz with me. Daniel leaned over me. "Are you awake, Din'ah?"

"Not sure." It took a few more blinks to focus past him. All my brothers stood around the bed, along with two of their wives. Stephanie and Olivia. And Casey, looking worried. "I guess so. Nothing like a little magic tea to knock you out."

Daniel moved away from the bed. "It's time. The women must prepare you."

I sat up. My body was whole again, but felt… fuzzy, slow. "I think there's still some residual effects from the drug."

"What drug?" Casey stepped forward.

Stephanie blocked him. "You can't touch her."

Casey stepped back, not about to push a woman out of the way, but his concern turned to annoyance. "Excuse me?"

"You can't touch her until after the ceremony." Joey slid up to Casey's side. "It's part of the next ritual."

"She's not even awake yet." Casey protested as Olivia helped me out of bed. "Are you okay, Beth?"

"I'm fine." My words were as slow as my body. Then I realized my Spirit was speaking to me, through me. I shook off Olivia's hand. "Nothing has started yet and his Spirit is pure. Leave us for a moment." I said it firmly enough everyone stepped backwards.

Daniel bowed to me. "The moon favors us tonight, an August Super-moon. Great power for the rituals."

How appropriate. "I only need a few minutes."

Casey waited until they left, the door closing behind them. He stepped towards me, ready to grab me, but held back. "They said I couldn't touch you while you were asleep, or… spirit walking? I don't know any of this. Are you okay? If not, say so and I'll put a stop to this."

"I was Spirit walking, and I'm all right." A step put me into his arms. "I'm going through something I can't really explain, but it's more of this transformation. I'm scared, but I understand why I have to do this."

"I think I do too. Your father tried to explain what to expect, about being the husband of a Ci'inkwia priestess. That this Spirit inside you is special among them. As special as you are to me. That I need to be strong enough for both of you, as you face the Maxa'xak."

"Wow, you managed saying all that without stuttering."

"I finally saw the video. I gave him my word I'd stand beside you, no matter what came at us, even that… thing. I intend to be there, no matter what."

"No." I pushed my head into his shoulder. "We're not married. You can still go and…"

"And what, pretend none of this happening?" Casey took my arms and pushed me back enough to make me look up at him. "I told you, I'm in this to the end, no matter what happens. No matter what they ask of me. I'm in this because I love you. I won't pretend that isn't real." He kissed me, hard.

I clung to him, kissing him back, wanting this moment to not end, but a rapping on the door and announced our 'couple minutes' was up. Casey didn't let go, holding me tighter. "I'm not going anywhere."

I refrained from pointing out that he was, that he had to leave now. Another rap on the door delivered the message. He let go, giving me one more kiss as Daniel knocked louder. “I’ll see you at the ceremony thing.”

As soon as the doors opened, Stephanie and Olivia brushed past him, Chucky wrapped an arm around Casey’s shoulders making sure he couldn’t come back. I couldn’t help but wonder if it was also to make sure Casey wouldn’t take off.

Olivia knelt over a trunk someone had delivered to the room while I slept. Three trunks in total. Stephanie pushed me towards the bathroom. She started drawing a bath, ordering me to undress. I wasn’t sure what they had in mind until Olivia joined us. She poured a golden oil into the water, then stirred it with eucalyptus branches.

The smell confirmed I was going to get a ritual cleansing bath. A bath to cleanse away any taint of the dark Spirits that crossed my path. As soon as the bath was full and steaming, Stephanie ordered me into it.

The water was so hot my flesh felt it was one degree from being burned off. The air was suffocating with the scent of the oil and leaves. I gasped as my body sank down into the water. Did my Star Spirit have control of my senses? Could my mortal body bear this?

The bath lasted nearly an hour, Stephanie and Olivia sang Navajo songs meant to drive away the evil they washed off my body. They waved feathers through the rising steam to dissipate any darkness I exhaled. Stephanie poured water over my head, the strong eucalyptus soaking into every pore, until they were certain I was purified.

Numbly, I followed a path of towels into the bedroom. Out the massive glass wall I could see the sun over the western mountains, almost ready to set. It was morning when we arrived at the hotel, meaning I'd slept most of the day. Dreaming. Spirit walking. I stared into the distance as they rubbed my body with more oil and braided my hair with wild Starbursts.

Normally I'd have objected to all this touching, especially standing in the middle of the room naked. But my Spirit expected this and held me there, perfectly content with the attention. This was all part of what was yet to come and she… I… was calm. I was prepared.

CHAPTER 22

They wrapped me in ritual clothes I'd never seen before. The white leather was velvety soft, nearly as thin as silk from age, and had a shimmer only accentuated by quartz bead where the fabric was woven together. I'd never seen these clothes with these eyes, but I knew their feel against my skin. She knew the feel.

Stephanie fastened the last shell button at my hip, stepping away from me. The leather molded to my every curve. Olivia set leather slippers in front of me, backing away as I tucked my feet into them, fitting as if made just for me.

Both women knelt down as the last rays of the sun blazed through the windows, casting shimmers around the room as they reflected off the crystal beads. They sang a Blessingway, but there were words I hadn't heard before, in a long time.

They sang to the Great Father and Mother, to the children of the gods, the Ci'inkwia left to battle for all the peoples. They sang a prayer to recognize and bless the offspring... to bless me, Din'ah, as a Star Woman. As the Ci'in.

Not a Ci'in, but the Ci'in.

They used my real name, her real name. Her real title. Even through the thick-paned glass, those rays of sunlight were a warmth glowing over me. Through me. My Spirit was alive. I took a deep breath, smelling eucalyptus, leather and Starbursts. Smelling life, as if for the first time in a very long time.

The song stopped as the sun disappeared. None of us said anything as they led me out of my suite and to the elevator. The guards stood statuesque, not a flinch of emotion, not the flicker of an eye as I passed between them. They took me to the rooftop, moving aside to let me step out alone.

But I wasn't alone. The roof had been designed as entertainment space, glass panels surrounding the perimeters for the safety of the guests. Any other time I had no doubt there were awnings with misters, tables, chairs and any sort of other special furniture for events. Right now furniture was replaced by people. At least a hundred, if not more.

They all looked at me, but I couldn't see anything except the display ahead of me. A structure stood in the middle of the roof. From four posts hung banners of the four Earthly Elements. Beneath each banner sat an Elder. Each Element and each Elder represented a conference of People. With all four Elders here, the entire Nation was considered present.

My heart thudded at the significance of this display. My father complained that even with Unity, it was difficult to get a full consensus. But they were here and in the center of the elders, sat a woman covered by a feathered robe. My mother.

Only I was surprised to see her. The Spirit expected it. My mother sat erect with her eyes closed, humming a tune I'd heard all my life. It was the tune she hummed in meditation. The song called to me, or to the Spirit within me. Flickering memories led me into the structure. I started to circle inside the structure, finally kneeling in front of an Elder.

Water. The Elder raised her head and I recognized her. She was the older version of my friend, Yazzie. Of course she would be first. Her tribe hosted this gathering. I bowed my head to her as she shook a water reed, sprinkling river water over me.

I expected it to be cool and refreshing, but instead each drop felt heavy. Each drop brought me memories of burdens I carried in my mortal life. Lives of soldiers and friends lost in the war. Lives of enemy combatants. The weight of the lives my decisions changed. The weight of Lutz' death. Even though I knew in my heart each of my actions were necessary, each drop was sorrow. Each drop a teardrop.

Earth was the next banner and an elderly man sang to me, dusting my body with what looked like glitter, but I could feel it wasn't plastic. Gold dust clung to my damp skin. Sparkling in the light and bringing to me thoughts of all the things I had pursued, not because of the things I needed, but simply wanted. Sometimes taking what I hadn't earned.

Not just possessions, but people, promotions, and the images I wanted others to have of me, whether they were real or not. I had fought my way into a misogynist society and pretended to be someone I really wasn't. I wasn't real in that world, or in this one, not with another being inside me. Who was I? I wanted to brush the gold off, but the song ended and the Spirit inside pulled me to the next Elder.

I went to Fire, afraid of what this Element would expose. A man my father's age twirled fire batons close enough to my skin they almost singed my flesh, but I was unharmed. Unburned, but feeling heat wash through me. The heat of lingering anger and resentments I'd buried deeper and deeper as I grew older.

Anger against prejudices because of my race, prejudices against my gender. Anger made me be a person I wasn't. I felt disappointment that my family didn't respect my choices, that I lost the bond I had with Frankie for so many years. I didn't know why. I even felt resentment towards Casey. He'd wanted me to return his love. I was afraid to let myself feel. Afraid it would make me weak.

These thousand wounds left by the first three Elements burned from the inside out. Stinging, I stumbled to the last Elder. I fell to the blanket beneath the Air banner. The woman was young, only a bit older than Daniel. She sang, her breath gentle against the pains left by Water, Earth and Fire.

Her voice was soft, but it carried a strength that said everything stopped to listen to her. Her song was light, but also sad, pulling at every regret, every sin, at every guilt. Tears streamed down my cheeks as she pulled them all to the surface. She looked upwards and my head tipped back too.

I stared up into a sky already dark enough for stars to flicker bright. Her song changed, to a prayer. If my Spirit was still strong, my mortal weaknesses would be washed away. If my Spirit was tainted with too much darkness, I would be rejected. My Spirit sang with her.

A burst of air washed down over me. It didn't pass as a breeze should, but swirled around me in a funnel. My body relaxed into the whirlwind, swaying with it, waiting for and accepting judgment. The breeze turned cold, embracing me. It grasped every pain the other Elements pulled to my flesh, blowing them away, cleansing my soul. Accepting me. Preparing me to face the Ci'inkwia priestess. My mother.

Circling the structure again, I felt no hesitation as I knelt before my mother. She still hadn't opened her eyes, nor stopped humming. Outside the four posts, people began to circle us. Those closest were the Ci'inkwia. They wore ceremonial robes with feathers attached at the hems and woven into their hair or headbands. They sang in the language we were never allowed to use in public.

They got louder as they danced, then all suddenly thrust their arms to the east. I looked and there was the moon rising over the mountains. The song and dance became a frenzy as the moon continued to rise, casting light over the rooftop. Once it was fully up from behind the mountains, they tapered off until they too only hummed, swaying to this sacred hymn.

With no dancers to distract me, I looked to my mother again. She opened her eyes, but what I saw in them wasn't the cheerful glitter I'd grown up to. "My daughter. Tonight you become the Ci'in and become leader of all our People."

She spoke to me, in English so that all in attendance could understand. "Before the final ceremony to free your true Spirit to this world, I must have a decision from your mortal being."

This part of the ceremony was in my Spirit's memories, I could feel it, but she wasn't sharing with me. It seemed important for me to face alone. It confused me. I'd already agreed to do this. "Please ask me, Mother."

She nodded. "We have been of this world for thousands of years, sharing mortal bodies and mortal lives. The only release from this world is battle with a Maxa'xak. Some Ci'inkwia may give so much of their energy to destroy our enemy, that their Spirit is too diminished to remain. Yet they may want to, if they have attached to a mortal."

My mother glanced to the star glittering in the south. The distant star flashed a little brighter. "Before every battle the Ci'inkwia must make the conscious choice, should this be their time."

A sound drew my eyes away from the star, away from the humming. The elevator doors opened and my father stepped out, followed by Casey. They had dressed him in little more than a breechcloth. I resisted laughing as he realized the roof was packed with people and he was almost naked. He dropped his hands down over the breechcloth.

CHAPTER 23

Casey stood silhouetted in the rising moon. He saw me and started to take a step towards me, but my brothers seized him. Casey tensed, but didn't fight them, instead glanced back at my father, who only nodded.

"Din'ah." My mother's voice called my attention back to her. "We are the children of the Great Father, of the Great Mother. We came from the stars to defend the people of this world from the Maxa'xak. We will face one of their kind soon in battle." Her eyes glistened. "As the Ci'in, it is your task to vanquish this Maxa'xak. If it is the last, our people will be free. All Ci'inkwia Unbound will be free to return to our home." Her arm drifted to the south star.

"Those who are Bound will live out their lives with their mortal mates. If this is truly the last Maxa'xak, all Unbound Ci'inkwia will leave this world."

She repeated herself, slowly. I heard what she said, but it didn't register. My Spirit showed me nothing. My eyes drifted to the flickering southern star, feeling a deep yearning to reach out to it. I looked to the first circle of dancers. Men and women mixed together. All Ci'inkwia. Dressed like my brothers, like my parents.

Behind them were the tribes we protected, the tribes we pretended to belong to. Stephanie and Olivia stood there, and their children. Married to Daniel and Frankie. Chucky's wife was here too, looking very pregnant. They were Navajo, but all my nieces and nephews looked like their fathers, like the Ci'inkwia. I never noticed that before.

An uneasiness crept into the calmness the earlier ritual had created. I looked to Casey. His expression looked odd, pained. What was he afraid of?

Suddenly I knew. I felt it as strongly as I felt the pull of that southern star. I had to choose. I had to choose now! "You are asking if I want to be married. If I know what will happen if I'm not when I face the enemy and kill him."

My mother nodded. "If you vanquish him, your Unbound Spirit will be released from the burden placed upon us. If he is the last of our enemy, all Unbound Ci'inkwia will be released."

I swung my head around to meet Casey's eyes again. "I've already given my promise to Casey. He is the man my heart is already… Bound to."

His fear disappeared and my mother gave a soft sigh. Her eyes glistened just a little lighter, just a little more of the woman I knew. She raised her arms to the sky, lifting her robe of feathers. "This woman choses to be Bound to an earth Spirit and live out a mortal life. They must be Bound now."

"Now?" I twisted around as my brothers tied a rope around Casey's waist. "What's happening?" I got no answer from my mother, or my Spirit, but the circle of

Ci'inkwia shifted. All the men stepped forward into a tighter circle as my father took the rope and pulled Casey into that circle.

I felt the brush of feathers as my mother was on her feet, stepping past me. She went to Casey, facing him, staring into his eyes. "Din'ah is to be the Ci'in. Only a mortal man of pure Spirit can marry one such as Din'ah, and survive when she comes into her full power. You are of pure Spirit. Are you pure enough of heart to be Bound to one of our kind? Strong enough to hold her to your world?"

Casey bowed his head to my mother. "My heart has always been Bound to Din'ah. It always will be and I will stand with her, as herself or as the Ci'in, in this and all challenges. I will stand with her and protect her until my own death."

"You must face the tribe, who will test your claim upon Din'ah." She stepped out of the circle and the song changed, to one of challenge. Each man withdrew an arrow from their quivers. I wanted to protest, but my Spirit prevented me from moving.

I was forced to watch as the men turned ferocious, screaming war cries as they lunged at Casey, jabbing him with their arrows. They drew blood, daring him to flinch, daring him to run. I suspected the worst of what would happen if he failed, but I knew my man. He didn't run from anything. He wouldn't run now.

Still, tears edged out as blood ran down his body. I could see his pain, even feel it, but he stood his ground until the song ended and the men withdrew. Casey looked ready to collapse. My heart ached for him, pounding hard in my chest. There were places where arteries ran close enough to the surface to be accidently nicked. Casey could bleed out and I was frozen in place.

Mother took the rope and the women stepped forward. They held long white feathers. I half-expected them to drive the quills into his flesh, but instead they started to sing our version of the Blessingway, brushing their feathers over his body. White feathers turned blood red, and with each flick of their wrists, Casey's wounds stopped bleeding.

Casey's obvious pain eased too, but he still looked exhausted as she brought him into the structure. She instructed him to kneel on the blanket behind me, but to not touch me. She released the end of the rope, then returned to the circle. She collected each feather. When she had them all, she raised the cluster to the moon and the Ci'inkwia all sang again.

She waved the feathers to the southern star. "The chosen mate has passed through the first two tests and is proven pure of Spirit, brave and true." She carried the feathers in front of her, back into the structure, with two elderly women following her. She laid the feathers in the space between Casey and myself. The two women knelt with the rope and feathers between them. Not looking at anyone or anything, but the feathers.

Mother returned to the place opposite me. "Din'ah. Daughter. This man is accepted by your family and by our tribe, but there is one final test you both must face. He must endure watching you suffer as your Spirit is completely brought to the surface. He must not touch you for any reason. He may only hold onto the rope that will tie you to him."

The two women behind me started humming a tune and from the corner of my eye, I watched as they tucked the quills of the feathers into the rope, one threading the feathers, the other separating the quill and using beads to bind the feathers to the rope.

Casey watched too, confused with what they were doing as well. He nodded to me and I looked back at my mother. “No touching. We understand.”

“No, you do not. Not yet.” She folded her hands over her chest. “I am of the blood. I am Ci’in, but I am not the Ci’in. That is decided by the Great Mother at the rebirth of every Ci’in. She marks that child and when she enters the Rising, it is of an intensity that some mortal bodies do not survive. There has not been a daughter with the mark for over a hundred years.”

The position of her hands on her chest told me what mark she referred to. A birthmark that somewhat resembled a starburst on my lower sternum.

“From your birth we knew you would face a Maxa’xak.” She waved her arms to the circle around us. “With other Ci’in, we saw signs of the Rising, but it has come on you so quickly that we had no time to help you integrate.”

Her eyes were getting that edge of fear in them again. “You and your Spirit must be integrated before you face battle and time requires we force the process. If your mortal body bears a weakness we have not seen, releasing her so suddenly can kill you.”

I heard Casey let out a gasp, but he didn’t move, as promised. My mother nodded to him, approving his self-control, but warning him too. “In this one night we must integrate you to your true Spirit. If you survive, then we will Bound you to Casey. But your Spirit must accept him too. If the rope is broken…”

“I will go into battle Unbound, and if I kill the Maxa’xak, I will die too.” I couldn’t sense my Spirit’s feelings towards Casey, only my own. “ I looked to Casey. “I will survive this and she will accept you. I promise.”

CHAPTER 24

"I'm ready."

The women behind me stopped their humming and lifted the rope. The blood-soaked feathers hung from it as they lifted the rope over my head.

My mother spoke up for everyone to hear her. "This woman chooses to be Bound by the blood of a mortal. He has sworn to stand with her for all his mortal time."

The women lowered the feathered rope in front of me, but held an end out to Casey. "Tie the rope strong, but do not touch her."

The rope settled around my hips. The feathers were still wet, brushing my legs and leaving stains on my skin and on the pearly white leather of my skirt. A flash of memory from my Spirit said this wasn't the first time.

"This man offers you his blood and pain. He ties the rope, but you will feel the weight of his commitment to you. If your Spirit breaks the rope, the Bounding will end. If your Spirit accepts, you will remain of this earth until your mortal body passes."

I felt the first twist of the rope. Casey didn't pull the rope tight, but the feathers grew heavy on my lap. My breath came harder. The second twist pulled the rope against my stomach.

The song began again, but with different verses. They sang of our home, of our free Spirits, of the freedom of the Ci'in and the Kwia. My Spirit drew me into the sway of the song.

I could feel the Rising. I could see who I'd once been. Completely alien, a completely different being. My Spirit ached in this mortal body and was drawn to that southern star. She wanted to look upon it once more. She want to go to that home.

But she had a duty to perform. She and all her brothers and sister. They had to remain here. It was more than an ancient task laid upon her. She had come to love this world, these people, and needed to save them. She needed to Rise and prepare for battle.

I needed to let her. I surrendered myself to the merging and felt the tug of the rope on my physical body as she rose to face that star. No. We were here to hunt down the Maxa'xak, every last one of them.

She turned to the eastern mountains. One existed there. Our mortal being had found it. We would kill it, then I could return home. If we failed we would be condemned to this world until the Great Mother selected another of her daughters to be the Ci'in.

I reached out to the star. Great Mother, please let us come home.

No! I turned to Casey. He gave her his blood, endured the pain as our people tortured his resolve. She gave him her promise, as he had given his.

No, she was me. My mortal-self.

The feathers were so heavy. I pressed them between my hands and thighs. Casey's blood smeared my mortal hands, burning them with his pain. The rope cut into me, even though it still hung loose around my waist. He held the ends as I gasped for air, he held onto her just as he'd promised to do for his short mortal life.

They were Bound together already, in that mortal way of their kind. But I wasn't. I couldn't be. A larger promise controlled me. They circle around me, singing of the life we once had, the life I would give back to them.

But her promise bore as much weight as mine. I felt the heaviness of so many promises. I looked to the priestess, her mother, confused. Why do I feel like this?

I already knew. I was of the stars, inhabiting a mortal body until my task was done. I couldn't make a promise to him. I didn't want to, but I couldn't deny this mortal vessel. Her desire to be with him bore as much weight as my desire to go home.

I wanted to go home. Where the sheer energy of the universe flowed through us as blood flowed through them.

"NO!" She screamed to be heard over the flood of my memories.

She made me look at Casey, but I only saw images of other men, of other times. The mortals I'd Bound myself to in other lives. I had learned to love them as did my mortal being, then watched them die. I wanted to go home, but…

"It is time to choose." I heard the priestess' voice and hands touched my mortal's skin. I stiffened, afraid he was touching me, but then saw it was other Ci'in. They laid me down on the blanket. My mother on one side, Casey on the other, still holding the rope in his hands.

The priestess chanted over me, blowing a smoke over my mortal body, into her face. I recognized the smell. Calea. With a few more puffs her breathing eased.

"Great. I hope this stuff is out of my system before I go back to work." I laughed. "Work, really? I'm about to go after a life-sucking demon from Alpha Centauri and I'm worried about a drug test?"

I didn't laugh. "The Maxa'xak aren't from Alpha."

"I know that!" "What?" My thoughts at the same time as hers. "Oh great, now we're both in here? I answered myself. Of course they weren't from Alpha. "Why are we here together?"

The answer was there as the schizophrenic split in my head continued, along with everything she ever knew. Thoughts rushed through my head faster than she could answer me, unless this was her answering me.

In the universe all things existed in a duality, light and dark, hot and cold, gentleness and brutality, Ci'in and Kwia, the Great Father and the Great mother. All things existed in balance. Countless life forces dependent on each other, yet so different, maintaining a careful balance. Any disturbance yielded either social lethargy or chaos, and ultimately, death.

But their careful balance wasn't perfect and after a millennia, dissenters Ci'inkwia found a dying species and merged their duality into those singular mortal beings. The Maxa'xak hybrids were fearsomely vicious and brutal, to the point of madness. They were also unable to propagate themselves. They needed suitable hosts to grow their larvae.

To find hosts, they ravaged worlds, creating such an imbalance, the Great Mother extracted a vow from her loyal children to put their wayward siblings out of their insane misery. We obeyed and we turned our powers against them.

The Maxa'xak knew we were capable of destroying them. Their survivors fled. We could have let them go, but we saw the death they left behind. If they reached another inhabited system, they would destroy whatever civilization existed there. If they found suitable hosts, they would bide their time, gain strength and return to wage war again.

We had given our vow and pursued them to this planet.

We found their ship, but the Maxa'xak were gone. They had found a water world, a primary element necessary for them to survive, and escape. Using the waterways, they scattered across the continent to find new hosts and start regrowing their horrific army.

The Ci'inkwia revealed themselves to the intelligent species of this world and learned of terrible beasts rising up from rivers and lakes, to snatch away anyone who wandered too close to the shores. Great serpents that primitive spears could not kill. This was what we sought, the Maxa'xak. We followed the stories, hunting them down one by one.

Fully enraged, the Ci'inkwia energy radiated hot, giving us the appearance of bird-like creatures who cast bolts of lightning down upon our enemy. We exposed our dual natures. The Ci'in and the Kwia, protective and merciless. Ci'in, the seekers. Kwia, the destroyers. Lightning and

Thunder. Thunderbirds. Our battles thundered across the countryside as we delivered death with no mercy to the Maxa'xak and their offspring.

One battle at a time, our war carried on from years to centuries, spreading further across the large continent, with no end in sight. To preserve our life forces, brave young humans sacrificed themselves to a select number of Ci'in and Kwia, creating a new People in the Nations. The Ci'inkwia. The Star People.

Those of our people not selected went dormant, sleeping until the first generation of children were conceived. Our Spirits transfer into those embryos, born into children, but sleeping until old enough to understand what we were, until old enough to battle a cluster of Maxa'xak. At which point one Ci'in was selected.

I was that Ci'in. I was the Ci'in. I had slept for over a hundred years, but I was awake again.

CHAPTER 25

I had lived so many lives. I had fought so many battles, but I had never vanquished a Maxa'xak. My sister had. I had seen her Spirit released. She had gone with joy, transformed back to pure energy. It was so beautiful, it hurt. The urge to return to my real form burned inside me. I willed my Spirit to Rise, but a weight pulled at me. My mortal body.

A small body, one I had slept within for many of her mortal years. I had slept until I felt the darkness of one possessed by a maturing Maxa'xak. Now I was awake. Now I would lead a battle against the Maxa'xak. The last battle. I could feel the energy of this universe, so close to being returned to balance. I had only to destroy this last obstacle and we could be free.

I had only to go out to find it. I tried to Rise, but a weight held me. A tether pulled me back. A rope attached to my waist. Hanging from that rope, feathers the color of blood. I was Bound?

My fingers ran over the rope and down the feathers, before letting my eyes follow the length. A man knelt at the other end of the rope, clinging to it as I floated above him. I could dislodge him with the flick of a thought, except I didn't.

I looked down at him, at the scars marking his body. Another memory returned. Her memory as she watched his blood turn the feathers red, whisking away the wounds he suffered, for her. I dropped closer to look at him more closely, with my own consciousness.

He had proven to have a pure Spirit. Born to replace an old Spirit that had reached ascension. It was good that these people were still capable of finding the path. It was good we had fought to save them.

I set my foot down upon the blanket where he knelt. He held firm of the rope, even though I no longer fought to be freed. His eyes stared at me with sheer wonder and a touch of fear. But not fear of me. Fear…

I leaned closer. I could almost touch him, but I didn't dare. In this state I might hurt him.

Staring into his dark brown eyes I knew his fear. He feared only one thing, losing the woman he'd Bound his soul to.

I'd seen this devotion many times. Love. These humans felt love. We felt love. Love was stronger than fear, stronger than desire, stronger than the pain of exile. I knew him and his love. I knew her love for him. Despite the yearning to go home, I couldn't deny her the one thing she truly wanted. I could not break her promise. We could not break a Bounding of this mortal love.

"I will not leave you, Casey."

Those words brought the full weight of the feathers onto me again, drawing me down to kneel before this man. A hand rose to his chest. My mortal's hand, overlain by the glowing mist that was me. My Spirit. I could feel this mortal's heart beating harder.

We were one, aware and integrated. I could feel his heart beat wildly against the mortal fingers I pressed to his bare skin. "I will be Bound."

"It is done!"

I didn't turn to look upon the priestess. I could see nothing but the face of the man before me. His fear was gone, replaced by an indescribable joy that matched hers. Nothing else existed except this bond between them, between us. I had resisted, but with the merging, I opened myself to all her emotions.

Nothing else existed. Not the stars, not the priestess, not the people who slipped through the shadows, leaving us alone. I slid my hand towards his face. He didn't pull away from a hand that wasn't the human he knew. He accepted the form I still held. He let me touch him, his body even trembled slightly as my hand slipped back down his chest, slowly.

I leaned into him again, this time letting my lips brush his, kissing him. I felt his hesitance and remembered he'd been told not to touch me. "The ritual is over, or almost..." I pressed my body against him. His hand grazed my leg, barely. I leaned into the kiss as his lips parted and pressed my leg against his hand.

His fingers slipped under my knee, drawing it around his leg. I wrapped my arms around his shoulders as his other arm slipped around my back. I might still be projecting my Spirit, but this body was fully conscious. The silk-thin leather of my skirt and his loin cloth did nothing to disguise his growing erection.

I tightened my arms and wrapped my other leg around him. He was quick to catch me, holding tight as I pressed against the heat spreading from both of us. "Make us yours. Now."

Casey's eyebrows furrowed together slightly and there was another moment of hesitation. "Who am I with? The Ci'in, Din'ah or Beth?"

I took a deep breath, which did nothing to ease the heat building inside this body. "I have always been Din'ah. I am the Ci'in to the Nations and in battle. I am Beth." I kissed him lightly letting her come through. "I am Beth."

Casey ran his finger along my cheek, then back into my hair, or what he saw as some semblance of hair. I knew what I looked like without a mirror to reflect the image he embraced. My ethereal overlay embraced the mortal body, making me humanoid, but her features were blurred out by the energy that comprised my Spirit. On this dark rooftop, I was nearly as bright as the moon above us.

But it didn't matter as I leaned back into his arm and he followed, laying me down onto the blankets. His lips went to my neck as his fingers untied the laces holding the scant shirt together. I might appear as light, but his hand had no trouble finding my breast.

Both mortal and immortal arched to the touch of his hand, rewarded by his tongue drawing circles around the hardened nipple. In full dark or blinding light, he knew this body well. Each touch, every flick of his tongue made me gasp in pleasure. "Only you ever made me feel like this."

"I know." His eyes looked up at me as his free hand untied my skirt, speaking between each pull of my breast between his lips. "And you… made me want you… as if my life and soul… depended on it."

His fingers went to the knot of the rope around my waist, but I closed my hand over his. "Not until…" I caught my breath as his body pressed harder against mine. "…I am yours."

Casey let go of the rope. He pulled at the narrow leather belt that held his breechcloth on. It unfastened and he pulled it free. "You were always mine." He kissed me.

I dug my fingers into his arms as he pushed deep inside me. We both groaned from the tightness of my mortal body. Anticipation was definitely an aphrodisiac. I arched this body as he devoured us completely with each kiss, with each thrust into this body. My human body shook with an orgasm, but I didn't let go of Casey.

He clung to us as he rolled over onto his back, carrying us with him. I wriggled this body down on him as he eased his hold. "I want to see all of my wife, so beautiful, both of you, under this moon."

I looked up. The moon was huge. Bigger than any moon I remembered. It was definitely a moon for such a sacred ceremony. I looked down at Casey, seeing it reflected in his brown eyes. I let go, giving him all of my Spirit and body.

At some point we became me again. Beth. I became the prominent being and he made love to me too, before carrying me down to our suite.

It must have been a sight for the guards as we exited the elevator. Casey had wrapped me in one of the blankets, but he was still naked. I snickered into his neck as he casually walked past them and down the hallway to our rooms.

CHAPTER

26

The curtains were drawn, but I could see the hint of light beyond them, telling me it was daylight, but I had no idea what time of the day. I was too tired to pull myself out of Casey's arms to look at the clock. I didn't want to. My whole body hummed from the inside out.

He must have felt my breathing change, raising up slightly to look at me over my shoulder. "Good morning, my dear wife." He smiled wickedly. "You have no idea how long I've wanted to say that."

"Yeah, I think I do." Even turning my head toward him was too hard to do. "I can't lift a finger."

"Really?" He laughed, kissing my shoulder, his hand cupping my breast as his hips started to grind against me.

"Oh my God. You've got to be kidding me." I let out something of an effort to laugh as I felt he wasn't just teasing. "Where is this coming from?"

"I think you… infused me with some of your energy." His kisses went to the spot behind my ear. "That or someone slipped an enhancer in the tea they fed me."

"Well, I can't stop you. Seriously can… not move… anything."

"No need to." He tugged his arm out from under my head, despite my groans. "A long bath and you'll be human…" He caught himself, laughing. "… or whatever."

I could see my hand on the pillow. It was the same rich golden shade it had been my whole life, before being possessed by my Spirit. "I'll just settle for alive." I let out a couple more groans as he slipped out of bed. Then heard the water running, which only lulled me back to sleep, until he came and picked me up out of bed.

I couldn't resist and didn't have a reason to as he lowered me into a perfectly warm and silky bath. My whole body let out a sigh, melting into the luxurious bath. Casey climbed in with me. Didn't care. Yes I did. He was my husband now.

"Husband." I repeated the word out loud, getting a kiss to the temple.

"Wife." He countered, his arms kept me from sliding away from him with all the oil he'd put into our bath.

A week ago I'd have done everything I could to get away from any conversation involving those two words. "I'm sorry."

Casey held me tighter. "For what? I got what I've always wanted." He nuzzled my ear. "We were meant to be."

I turned my head to lay it on his shoulder. "I know. I just feel like I put us through a lot of torture to get here.

Especially when I never felt so at peace with anyone in my whole life."

"I'm going to make sure you never feel any differently." He stroked my arm. "You had a choice, to be free or Bound to me. I saw what you are, inside. I felt it… when you were… transitioning. I felt your yearning." His voice broke and I could see the knot in his throat rolling. "You gave that up to stay with me."

"She did, or rather only postponed it." I corrected him.

"You have to live the rest of your life mortal." He laid his head down on top of mine. "For a few seconds I felt what that meant and I almost let go of the rope. You… she was so beautiful, something that should be free. Not like us. But then she looked at me. I don't know what she saw, but it broke and mended my heart, at the same instant, when she said she'd not leave me."

"And we won't."

I cozied up to him, feeling as close now as when we'd made love. I must have nodded off again, but Casey kept my head above water. It was still warm, the water heated by the jets, but I woke to see my fingers all wrinkly. I could also move again, somewhat. Casey helped me out of the bathtub.

Every muscle in my body was fatigued. I knew it was from the Rising ritual, but it was a lot more fun to blame Casey. He grinned and blushed at the same time.

I crawled back into bed. Whatever was going to happen was going to have to give me recovery time. A factor I was sure all Bound Ci'inkwia knew. I curled up in a pile of pillows, under the thick duvet, just breathing. Just sleeping, lost in Casey's arms.

I barely woke the rest of the day. I was a bit surprised no one bothered us, but I really was in no shape to go to battle yet. At some point I stirred enough to realize I hadn't eaten more than a half sandwich in two days. Casey ordered from the penthouse menu, then finally let the day in by opening the curtains.

It was evening already. The sun was dipping towards the western sky, but there was enough daylight left to invade our sanctuary. It also illuminated something else. "What the hell is that?" I sat up as Casey turned around in the light.

He had marks up his arms and down to the middle of his chest. Marks that weren't there before and they weren't the arrow scars. Those scars were gone, replaced by a design. I opened my mouth to demand an answer, but the memory returned. "I did that to you."

"Yeah." He looked down at his chest. "It burned a bit at the time, but it doesn't hurt." He came to sit next to me, catching my hand as I tried to trace the markings from his arm to his chest. "I'm a marked man." He threw in a wink.

My Spirit did this to him in a moment of passion. Hers burned just as intensely as my own as she spread those wings of energy across Casey, proclaiming him the life-mate of the Ci'in?

I stroked the wings of a great bird and my body trembled. Casey caught my hand in his, looking a bit pale for a flash of a second, then laughing nervously. "Wow, that's not…" He sucked in a breath. "As much as I'd like you to not stop doing that, now's maybe not the best time to see what happens."

His body said otherwise, his boxers not too successful at hiding his arousal. I was tempted, but steadied myself and pushed him away. "You're right. We…" A knocking on our door worked at squashing the urges we were both feeling. Casey jumped from the bed, grabbing a robe as he went to the door. He open it slightly to peek out into the main salon.

Stephanie stood discreetly to the side of the door, so as to not catch a glimpse inside. “Ci’in, I brought your food.”

“Thank you, Stephanie.” Casey opened the door completely and grabbed the cart, pulling it inside the room.

“I am also to tell you of a council meeting at nine tomorrow.”

“Noted.” Casey lifted a lid off one of the plates. “I’ll make sure she’s ready.”

She nodded, without looking at either of us. “Is there anything else you require?”

“Stephie.” I called out from the bed. “I appreciate the heads up, but you’re my sister-in-law, my sister, not my servant.”

Her body turned further away from the door. “You are Ci’in. You’re THE Ci’in. Highest of all the Ci’inkwia. They bow in your presence, so must I.”

The awe in her voice was heartbreaking. “No. I’m still me, Beth, Daniel’s baby sister. Look at me.” She shifted her eyes towards me. “See, not glowing or anything weird. We’re still family.”

She nodded, though remained withdrawn. “I’ll try to remember that. Is there anything else you need?”

I held in the exasperated sigh. “No, thank you.” Casey eased the door shut as she turned away. “Not too sure I’m going to like this idol worship thing. I haven’t even done anything yet.”

"Normally I'd agree with you, but after seeing what was on your camera, and seeing what happened last night, you've been crowned their leader, babe."

He pushed the cart to the side of the bed. "Let's get some food, then I'll let you play with my new tattoo."

Our dinner was real short.

CHAPTER

27

Casey kept his word to Stephanie, making sure we were up in time for the morning meeting. I was a lot stronger and ready to face them, though I wasn't rushing. I lingered on the side of the bed while Casey started opening closet doors. Inside were clothes, new clothes. Two rods holding his and hers outfits.

"Where'd all that come from, and when?"

"Yesterday, when you were sleeping." Casey started dressing. "Joey only grabbed us a change of clothes and the stuff from our safe. Your computer, Lutz', the guns, papers, anything someone might want to get their hands on."

"Good." Inspired, I started going through the closet. A cabinet door on the side held the guns, everything I hadn't taken with us into the mountains. Casey's guns, hunting and assault weapons he didn't keep in the armory. We were well armed.

Computers, valuables from the safe, passports. I locked the cabinet again.

I pulled out a crisp new pair of black Levis, a matching tank top and from a drawer removed brand new underwear. I gave Casey a roll of the eyes.

He laughed. “I only told them your sizes. You have to blame their wives for the selections.”

“I’m sure!” He often tried to supplement my ‘military practical’ style with stuff he liked. I waved the push-up bra at him. “Really?”

He grinned. “If your sparkling personality doesn’t charm them, your ta-tas will.” I swatted him with the bra as he pulled on his new black Levis. He bent down and gave me a quick kiss. “Quit complaining and get dressed. I’m starved.”

He always had a thing for being a bit matchy-matchy. His cowboy-tight Levis and snug tank top displayed his chiseled muscles, front and back. I loved his arms and now with the way the Ci’in tattoo laid over the bulging triceps…

I turned away to dress before my imagination got any more lurid. There was power over him in those tattoos and it didn’t take much for me to take advantage of that fact. I dressed quickly. The Levis fit perfect. He liked them a bit tighter, but I needed to be able to move. The shirts were simple, a black tank underneath a white women’s oxford. All new and crisp.

At least they didn’t replace my favorite cowboy boots, worn to the point that my pinkie toes threatened to pop out through the leather. I’d had them since high school and resoled them at least three times. They had a good half-tread still on them, treaded for desert terrain.

I tied off the shirt as someone knocked on the door again, followed by Stephanie's voice. "Your breakfast is set up in the salon."

I rushed to the door, but she was already disappearing out of the suite. I let out a sigh, backing into the room again. "Go ahead and get started while I finish up."

"Appreciate it." Casey slipped around me. "I'll save you something."

"Do that." I headed to the dressing table and finished brushing my hair. It still smelled of eucalyptus, and was soft from the oil. I was lingering again, then nearly jumped out of my skin when an apparition appeared behind me in the mirror.

I spun around. "Lutz! Really?" I wanted to reach out to try touching him, but knew it would be pointless. "I'm not dreaming or under the influence. So you can just show up anywhere now?"

He grinned. "Yeah, kinda. You didn't have all your abilities to see me before, so that was my only choice"

"Well, now I do, and if you haven't noticed, this is the bathroom. My bathroom, in my bedroom. Like, did manners die with you?" I grimaced as I heard myself. "Sorry."

Lutz shrugged. "No offense taken. And I listened before entering, since I haven't learned to knock yet." He silently rapped on the door. "I'm still in Ghost 101. Knocking and chain rattling comes in Haunting 210."

"Okay, I'll give you that one." I rolled my eyes at him and got up from the dressing bench. "So what's up? You here to deliver some prophetic message?"

"Wow, testy are we? I'd have thought you'd be all mellow today."

"Ewww, you just said you didn't peep."

He laughed. "Partner, I didn't even try to listen, but that hooting and howling was enough to wake the dead..." He paused, looking down at himself. "Well, maybe not. Still dead."

"Don't do that." I closed my eyes, his image at the bottom of the cliff something I'd never forget. "Joking doesn't make this easier."

"Sorry. I didn't come here to upset you." I felt a pressure on my arm, a stroking, but I didn't open my eyes. "I'm not really dead. There is an afterlife, but I need to be a part of this battle, before you release my soul. So don't torture yourself."

His touch was comforting and I dared to look at him again, though my throat knotted tight. "I have to explain this to Sabrina."

Lutz pulled his hand away. "Yeah, that sucks, but she knew she was marrying a soldier and bad shit happens. By now she'll be wondering why she can't reach me." He eased away, clearing the door to let me out of the bathroom. "Maybe before you release me, I'll pay her a visit, try to ease the impact."

He followed me across the room. "I promise I'll do whatever I can to help."

"I know you will."

I went out into the main room. Lutz still following me.

Casey looked up from pouring coffee and spilled half the pot all over the table. "What the hell?"

I stepped away from Lutz, glancing between them. "You can see him?"

"Shit!" Casey started grabbing napkins from the service tray as coffee started dripping off the table. "Yeah, I can." He tried sopping up coffee, but couldn't take his eyes off Lutz. "You're dead!"

"What?" Lutz started slapping his chest, looking totally horrified. "I am?"

"Knock it off." I headed to the other side of the table, using more napkins to soak up a run-away trail of coffee, shaking my head at Casey. "It appears death unleashed a twisted, not-so-funny, sense of humor."

"I am too funny." Lutz acted offended, then shrugged a shoulder. "Sorry to freak you out, dude. Apparently I'm not the only one who went through a change. Normally YOU shouldn't be able to see me."

Casey rubbed his chest, turning away only enough to grab a bar towel. "I'm sorry about what happened to you. Is there a reason you're… here?"

"Wow, dude! Thought we were friends." He gave me a wink.

"He's tied to me until I do a ceremony to release his Spirit. He wants to help, somehow."

"Well, however I can." Lutz lingered as I took one of the chairs. "I went out to my body when they came to get it. Yazzie and her people made it look like they picked up two bodies. She fed the coyotes and they disappeared down the gulch. By the time they'd loaded up the bikes, the bad guys had shown up. Yazzie's people pretended not to see them as they took off."

"And they didn't get shot at?"

"Almost. A couple of the guys took aim, but the pack leader said it would draw too much attention if anymore locals disappeared. Plan is to lay low until after the Marines come out to investigate." Lutz nodded at me. "Actually he seemed a little sad that you were dead. Think he'll be planning to come to our funerals?"

I rubbed my face with both hands. "Dude, really, the information's useful, but don't know how much more I can take of you talking about being dead so nonchalantly, as if it's a joke."

"Well!" Lutz got up abruptly. "I know where I'm not welcome."

"No, wait…" Casey looking confused, worried. "… um, ah, geez. What am I supposed to say? Beth didn't really mean to offend you?" He sounded completely unsure.

Lutz laughed, grinning. "Just messing with ya. I just dropped by to say I'd be around. You just have to think about me and I'll know you want to chat."

"Okay…" Casey still didn't sound sure, but then it wasn't every day one found themselves talking to a ghost. "So, before you go… If you can just show up wherever, can you go spy on the bad guys for us?"

"No. Sorry." Lutz shook his head. "Already tried. Can't go anywhere I haven't been, unless there's someone I know there. We tend to haunt people, not places." He raised a hand and snapped his fingers, disappearing.

"Yeah, cute, dude. The special effect wasn't necessary."

CHAPTER 28

Casey squinted at me. "So he's just going to pop in whenever he feels like it?

"Of course not." I reached across the table to pull one of the overfilled coffee cups my way. "He eavesdrops first, until he learns how to knock."

"Okay, that makes me feel sooo much better." He switched to the other side of the table from the mess. "So he can't go find out what this…Maxa'xak is up to?

"Nope." I sipped at the coffee, complimented by the array of flavored creamers room service sent up. "I'm not exactly sure why he can't be released until I do it. It's… disturbing. Bad enough I got him killed in the first place, but he might come in handy somewhere."

"That is disturbing. Fighting an alien monster with a ghost."

“Well, the Maxa’xak won’t expect it.” I shook my head. “What he can do remains to be seen. Eat. We have a meeting to go to.”

There was plenty to choose from off the breakfast cart. Casey ate with a ravenous gusto, while I nibbled. My mind kept going to the meeting as the minutes got closer.

Casey slurped down the last of the coffee. “I guess it’s time. You’ve switched the soldier back on.” He pushed away from the table. He’d always said I did that when it was time for me to head to base. “May I escort you, Capt. Castle?”

“You mean Delgado now. We’ll have to fix that when this is over.” I got up, taking one more bit from a biscuit. “Let’s go see what the plan is.”

The officer in me wanted to pat my hip for my Sig, but it was safely locked in the cabinet. Casey pressed his hand into the small of my back, urging me to go. He didn’t let up pushing me down the corridor and into the elevator, then down to PH3. A short ride, but my stomach knotted up. Casey must have felt my tension, his hand spreading out over my back. “You’ll be fine.”

“Yeah.” I tightened my shoulders. I was about to face a bunch of soldiers, but not the ones I was accustomed to. These were the Ci’in and the Kwia. A wave of memories flowed through me. These were warriors and I was their leader.

The elevator doors opened and I stepped out without Casey pushing or dragging me. There were more of my kind here. I could feel their energy and let it draw me across the penthouse lobby to a set of ornate doors. They opened before I reached them, Daniel and Frankie, bowed their heads to me. I stepped into the large board room.

It was a packed room. The energy of all the Ci'inkwia washed over me. I didn't ask, just walked to the empty space at the head of the table. Joey waved Casey over to join him in the chairs circling the room. I stood there, staring into the faces of my kind as well as local tribal leaders high-ranked enough to be included in this battle. *Lucky them.*

"Shall we begin?"

They were ready. Yazzie's tribe provided holographical maps of the mountains where the enemy camp was. Most of the mortal tribal leaders from the region were present, along with the four Elders. Next to my mother was a tribal leader from the Great Lakes Algonquians. Looking at him I could see where we got our mortal genetic material. It was their men and women who made us members of their tribe. If this was the last battle for us, it was fitting they be here.

After pointing out the location of the Maxa'xak, and showing the video, a basic attack plan was laid out. Every battle had the same anchor strategies. Using those guidelines, we divided into action teams.

We needed to get all our people in place at night, while the moon was still so large and bright. We knew the wash routes were going to be watched closely, and something had set off an alarm to let them know we'd reached the ridge over the encampment.

An old Cocopah leaned over the holographic display. "My people have hunted these mountains for centuries. We know paths no one else knows. Paths no one should follow." He poked his finger into the hologram, where my photos had been merged to show the enemy installation. "My grandfather warned us to stay out of this area. Stories tell of ghosts miners who steal the souls of wanderers. We did not suspect the Maxa'xak. No waters flow there."

"An understandable conclusion. We heard some of the same stories and explored a number of mines for possible underground water sources." My father nodded towards my brothers. "We've explored Recluse Goatherder's, Death Valley Scotty's, Lost Dutchman and a dozen others, but none yielded the quantities of water needed for a Maxa'xak."

One of the Kwia from California moved around the table to look into the hologram more closely. "Even with another ten thousand years we couldn't search every nook and cranny on this continent."

"Being the middle of a desert, we assumed the Tinajas would yield the same results, so we've been focusing on other areas. Why is it here, in these particular mountains? Do we have any better geo-surveys?"

Someone pulled up more maps, satellite geo-formation maps used to monitor aquifers in agricultural areas. "The processes have gotten better since they started this, but the mountains are probably too dense for the scans."

Movement drew my attention away from the table. Casey had left the spot where he'd been quietly listening. He came up behind me. Eyes all shifted to him and he froze. "Sorry, not to interrupt, but I have a question."

"Of course. You know this area, these mountains."

Casey shrugged. "Well, maybe it's a stupid question, but if this thing's been here for ten thousand years, why is it only on this continent. Why not Mexico, South America, or migrated to China or Russia? There's a lot of water on this planet."

"It's not a stupid question." I looked around the room to see non-Ci'inkwia raising eyebrows here and there. "It just hasn't been asked in a long time."

I waved my hand at the tech handling the electronics. "Take this away and show the Maxa'xak."

The hologram turned into the ugly snake creature that slithered out of the building. The tech froze it in the upraised position. The image exposed short appendages, looking like clawed paws, intended to hold down prey. It was poised over the humans, giving a good size scale. It had horrified my mortal side, but sickened my Ci'in.

"As you can all see, they are as large as their myths. However, their mobility is limited. So migration outward from their initial landing site was slow." That got a few half-hearted nods from outsiders. "We also found out that they can only tolerate fresh water sources. Salt water is toxic to them, as in battery acid toxic. That was probably a huge disappointment for them, but a blessing for the planet. If they get within fifty miles of a coastline, just the higher saline in the air starts burning them."

California confirmed that info with a nod. I could see he wanted to speak, so I relented the floor to him. He stood up. "They landed in the northeast shortly after the Clovis event. They would have left the planet in search of another suitable world, but their ship had reached its limits. The ship had enough energy cells left to prolong their stasis, so they slept as the continent recover. With the Folsom period, tribes arrived to resettle the Great Lakes area. That's when they came out of stasis, spreading out and beginning propagation."

"And it's about the time we arrived." My father spoke up. "They had scattered through the river systems by then. We found a few dead along the east coast and down in the gulf. Killed by the salt water."

"The rest of them evaded us, making the hunt last for thousands of years. We were close to winning..." My mother spoke, her voice so mournful. "…until white people started migrating to this country. The population went up quickly, but whites had no appreciation for anything outside their one God. They created another level of threat. The Maxa'xak gave up their eastern hunting grounds and headed west."

I saw Casey's mouth open, but the Algonquin cut him off. "They went west because the north was too cold for them. The west was lightly populated and still innocent in their beliefs."

"But not for long. Human migration and a quickly changing environment kept pushing them further and further west. We pursued the few that remained, evading the growing conflicts between the tribes and the new invaders. Even as the People were driven onto the reservations." My mother looked to the Algonquin. "We kept a low profile and our pursuit."

"It was understood our battles were not yours." He bowed his head to her.

I remembered those years, the agony we felt as our friends were killed and oppressed. "Those times have finally passed and our war is close to ending."

Casey nodded as he considered my last words. "So we have to keep it from reaching a third-world environment."

"Which is probably why it's here. It has a constant flood of hosts that no one will miss." I finished his thought.

My father leaned on the table. "And it's been here amassing the means to move further south. The vehicles, a helicopter, a small army of infected subjects. This location is now no longer safe, but it has to have a new hunting ground located before it attempts to leave."

"Which means we have to take it out now, in case it's already located a new hide-out. So we need to get on with the plan." It was a bit less subtle than normal for me. My Spirit was getting anxious with the history lesson.

"Yeah, I get the migration and urgency, but…" Casey still looked unsure and didn't back down. "I still don't get the repopulation thing. Why are there only this handful of zombie-host men?"

My mother winced at the term and I regretted sharing that reference with Casey. She answered for me. "It takes over a hundred years for a single larvae to mature and humans haven't proven to be prime vessels. Out of a hundred people, only one or two might accept the larvae. Then it has to actually survive to maturity."

I looked around the edges of the room to the mortals. "You humans have done a good job at rejecting the larvae, keeping reproduction levels down." They didn't fully appreciate the compliment.

Mom took over again. "Once the larvae are introduced, they produce the hormones and cells needed to keep the body regenerating so they can live to maturity. Unfortunately the human brain is destroyed, creating what Casey calls zombies. These creatures aren't good at maintaining control, so they rely on the telekinetic-type energy of the host."

"Basically, they're rather stupid. Hence zombies." My mother didn't look at me, knowing the reference came from her, not Casey.

"Yeah, so if you run into a zombie, zombie-kill it. Cut out the heart, blast out the guts, blow off the head, whatever is so catastrophic the larva can't regenerate the body. You will be giving the host their final mercy."

CHAPTER 29

With Casey's questions answered, we went back to plotting our way into the mountains. Our Cocopah hunter marked out the old paths. We had to hit the enemy from different sides, drawing out the Zombie soldiers, but also making sure none of them could make a run for it.

A nudge at my arm warned me before Lutz whispered in my ear. "I can go to the Zombie camp, but not inside. With me there as a lookout, I can report if they start coming your way too soon." I gave him points for not materializing in a room where half of us were in touch enough with Spirits to see him.

"We need to narrow down the approach. Both times we set off some type of tripwire." I drew lines through the hologram of our routes in, then out, speaking to Lutz, but having everyone's attention. "Probably the same technology that lets them know when a group of illegals are close enough to grab."

"Border Patrol uses infrared and motion monitors along the border." The head of the Cocopah Reservation Police looked to Casey.

"We do, but not everywhere. The Tinajas area hasn't had the influx to justify the expenditure." Casey raised a hand to stop any comments before they started. "I know. Just because the government approves the aid stations doesn't mean they'll give me funds to improve our monitoring systems."

"That's true. Our funding comes from the UN under humanitarian aid, not law enforcement or immigration. We don't get any funds for monitoring. But apparently they have the funds. Question is where…"

The old hunter pointed at the hologram just as I lifted my hand. "Here and here." He touched on two mountain tops. "They are the only points from where they could see you coming into their area, but not the ascent to the ridge. If you had stayed on the same path…" He didn't need to finish that sentence. Lutz gave my shoulder a comforting stroke.

"Makes sense. Using those points, give me routes in. Give me an exact location of their monitors. We need to disable them to make our way in."

I quietly let the old man and the computer tech launch into a virtual search for the locations of the presumed sensor arrays. They kept moving their 'all-seeing eyes' up and down the sides of the two mountain until they found the area where the one path was fully obscured. They overlapped the new map with the old hunter's paths.

Joey stepped up to the new display. "That's our ways in. Not pretty."

Having my attention, I came around to the perspective Joey had. "And that's if these are the only two arrays."

"Oh, no doubt there's more." He pointed around the table. "These are primarily for hunting prey, not self-defense. Other sites will be covering the rest of the mountain range."

Daniel joined us too. "We need to get their escape route covered, so we need to come in from this angle." He pointed to the plateau and the only way off it. "One team has to get here. Another needs to come in from the top. We need to take these arrays out to get in there."

"No we don't." Joey ran his finger along an old trail that ran nearly parallel the natural wash, but hidden from the array. However, it had most of the wash covered. "This is the one that got you going in the first time. You can get this far without being detected if you follow this trail. It'll get you close to the base of the plateau. By then we'll have started the first offensive."

Daniel shook his head. "Too much rough ground to cover in the interim. And there's the matter of us getting our warriors into their positions."

"Not if we take out this array." Joey pointed to one of the targets. "Shut this down, please."

The tech complied and the gap between the trail and the bottom of the plateau opened up. So did a few others higher up the mountain.

"There's no doubt they'll have something to cover the way you went in, recognizing it as a gap in the array overlaps, but taking this array out will get the ground team to their assault point, and the upper assault team to their rappelling points." Joey grinned. "And it's the easiest to reach. I can get up there and shut it down."

"Shutting it down might alert them."

Joey gave Daniel an annoyed frown. "This is my specialty. I can make it look like a glitch, delayed feed, cutting out sections where our teams have to cross through."

"And I can help with that." Our tech expert put himself on Joey's team.

"Sounds good. Work it out."

I expected an argument from Daniel, then remembered I now outranked him. "Daniel, with this information, you and Frankie finalize your assault plans. Chucky, you get to head up my team, ground level assault. Mom, Dad, we'll need support teams, logistics, medical triage… you know the routine and who needs to run the details."

I wasn't picking family out of preference, but out of experience. This was our region. "You have an hour before we present." I joined Chucky as he gathered our team. I didn't ask about his selection. Years of hunting with my brothers taught me a lot. It was one of the few times I didn't argue with them.

I didn't need to argue with anyone on this mission. I was cargo, a weapon they had to get to the front line. So I listened as he laid out everyone's duties.

At the end of the hour the teams all reported their individual plans. As the details turned to support efforts, I felt sluggish. Maybe I should have eaten more. I needed energy, and soon. The effects of Rising were always this way, physically draining and a bit confusing as mortal and immortal minds coalesced.

My mother's voice snapped me back. "… for today. Group leaders can finish this. Submit your supply requests and we'll have everything ready by dinner." She shifted my direction. "The Ci'in needs to complete her recover and prepare, in order to be ready for this assault."

"We need to prepare also." Her eyes moved around the room, looking at every face there. "If this truly is the last Maxa'xak, our time here is over. Those Unbound will depart. If that is not their wish, they must be Bound tonight." She touched my father's arm. "It has been ten thousand years. Everyone should be prepared. Make sure all our People understand."

No one protested, getting up and silently leaving, except my family. My mother looked at my father and his hand covered hers in a touch I didn't see very often. A silent message none of us could hear. I caught Daniel watching too, with an expression of sadness, before he dropped his eyes. He wrapped an arm over Joey's shoulders.

My heart pounded with a sudden fear. My Ci'in confirmed the growing thought in my head. My parents were both Ci'inkwia, so there was no ceremony to Bound them together. And Joey was unmarried, without children. I wanted to jump to my feet, but my legs felt weak, as if all the blood drained out of my body.

"You're leaving me!"

My mother tore her eyes away from my father's. "If this is the end, we'll be free." She still held his hand. "In the mere blink of an eye, you and your brothers will join us."

My Spirit knew this, but my heart didn't care. Casey's hands gripped my shoulders. I didn't get emotional often, but he always seemed to know when I was on the edge. She noticed, smiling at him. "You won't be alone and your children will never carry this burden."

Children? I'd never even thought of that. "But you won't be here to help me raise them." I couldn't stop the tears from welling up on my bottom lids.

My brothers weren't doing much better, fighting their own emotions. Joey kept running his hand over his chest, as if something inside was already splintering apart. He looked at me with such sadness. "Joey…"

Father stood up. He was normally such a quiet man, but when he spoke, you listened. "Bound or Unbound, no mourning. We are not dying, only transcending this world for our true existence. You will one day join us."

My mother pushed her chair out and my father helped her stand. She came around the table. I stood up, but she reached for Casey. He stepped forward, accepting her embrace. She took his hand and folded it into mine. "You won't be alone."

"No, she won't." He looked past my mother to the rest of my family. "I can't say I fully understand this, but I'll do my best to make the transition easier."

Mom focused on me again. "This is only tragic to your mortal self. You need time to finish remembering your full Spirit, maybe meditation. There is a place by the river." She glanced to the windows. "Take the rest of the evening and let us worry about what tomorrow brings."

"Mediation's not going to help. Besides, I don't know how to meditate the way you do." Her meditation went so deep that we joked the house could burn down around her, but if we did anything wrong, she knew.

She gave me her 'I know better' smile and stroked my cheek. "Now that you have Risen, it will come to you, Din'ah. Let go of your defenses and you'll remember."

"I'll try." I resisted reaching out to hold onto her as my father came and pulled her away from me, leading her out of the conference room. My brothers followed them out, circled around Joey.

I leaned into Casey. His arm tightened around me as I pressed my face to his chest. "I know what they say is true, but I can't help feeling like I'm leading them to their deaths. I've done this a thousand times. It shouldn't hurt like this."

"Then let's go do what your mother says. Center yourself." With a nudge he started me out of the room. At the elevator we waited just a moment before it returned. Casey called Cherise, telling her where we wanted to go.

She met us as the doors opened on the ground floor, holding a blanket folded over her arm, looking completely calm as if we hadn't called her only seconds before. "I'll take you down to the riverside. We have a private beach for our penthouse guests."

"Thank you." Casey wrapped his arm around me. "Is it possible to bring us some food and drink?"

"I have already ordered a basket to be brought to the beach. If you'll follow me."

She led us out the private rear entrance, across the circular drive and into a desert garden with Spanish pavers creating paths that split off into different directions. She took us to the right, towards a tall, ornate, wrought iron fence.

A noise behind us drew my attention. Two large security guards. I hadn't seen them join us, which probably proved they were good.

Cherise stopped at the fence, using a card key on a gate key pad. “You will have total privacy here.” In a few steps one guard reached for the gate, holding it open for us while the other guard covered our backs. We left the garden and moved into a grove of trees.

I could hear the river, even smell it. We didn’t have far to go before we stepped into an area filled with white sand, leading to a small cove. Turning back towards the hotel, it was almost invisible through the trees. “This is nice. Quiet.”

Cerise gestured to the gazebo under the trees. “You should find everything you need there. Anything else is but a call away.” She bowed and left us.

Casey went to the gazebo, the back wall enclosed with stocked cabinets and a beverage cooler. He removed beach blankets and a couple beers. “Let’s just relax. If you feel like doing meditation, it’ll come to you.”

“I think I want a swim first.” I took a blanket and headed towards the water. Modesty made me give a good look around before I stripped down to my underwear. “A swim and some sun, then maybe…”

As wound up as I felt, I doubted I’d ever achieve the right calm, so I needed to use whatever I could to relax and not thing about how tomorrow would bring battle, and blood, and heartache. I ran into the water, plunging in, hoping the shock of cold water would distract me.

I took my time rising back to the surface. Gasping for air when I did. The cold water helped rinse away the gloomy mindset. Casey peeling off his clothes helped too. I liked the sunlight on his new tattoo. “Hurry up. Husband.”

He grinned as he stomped through the sand and into the river. Thoughts of battle did not last long.

CHAPTER

30

I stared out the truck window as we headed down the range road. Casey drove. He knew the route as well as I did. It was still dark, but we had to be in place by daybreak, when we would attack the Maxa'xak lair and kill it. Kill all those it had implanted with larvae, and hopefully rescue the captive illegals before they became hosts.

I wished there wasn't anyone needing rescue. The fewer witnesses the better.

"You alright?" Casey reached across the console to take my hand.

"Yeah." I gave his hand a squeeze back. "Just getting my head into the game. Kind of strange how different a hundred years or so can make it, but it still be the same. We both have better weapons, but it all evens out."

"Wouldn't call it even. Not if he's the last one."

"I mean the universe. I can feel the universe on the edge of balance. It's the first time in eons. We're almost done." I turned back to the dark desert. One more night had completed the merge between us. My senses were prickly sharp. My emotions were stable and memories flowed at my bidding, not hitting me like bricks.

Glancing over my shoulder I could see my father also watched our lights cast shadows over the desert. My mother was no longer able to fight, but he was still robust for his mortal self. He'd do triage on the plateau, she'd be liaison for the after-effects.

There would be wounded, as well as deaths. She and other older Ci'in would be Spirit Vessels, holding the Spirits of our fallen until they could be released. What happened after that depended on whether we won or lost.

Fingers closed tighter around my hand and Casey gave me a slight nod. I must have been broadcasting my worried vibe. He knew me so well, even though I was now such a different person.

Or was I? Right now I was ten thousand years old and feeling my age, praying this would be over. The other part of me wasn't even thirty yet, and wanted desperately to stay here forever, with Casey.

"The site's straight ahead." Casey slowed as I pointed ahead at the mobile shelter stuck up under a row of mesquites. "We'll off-load the bikes here and go in. The path will be narrow and dangerous."

Chucky threw me an eye roll. "Been doing this as long as you have, Sis."

"Yeah, but the last time was on horseback." It sounded weird saying that out loud.

"Here we are." Casey said it a bit louder than necessary, interrupting what was about to turn into a sibling spat. Our fifth passenger let out a single huff of laughter. Casey circled the truck and pulled to a stop.

We piled out, Casey jumping into the back of the truck and unfastening the straps holding the dirt bikes in place. Chucky and the other Kwia did the offloading. I studied the trailhead the old hunter had sent us to. Entry was almost a mile from the military route we used to check the aid stations, but ran almost parallel.

Parallel until the washes merged. This path transected the smaller tributary just north of where Lutz and I had been stopped. I checked my watch. We could get part of the way to our target using the blind spots the mountains created. By the time we were out of cover, Joey and his team would have the sensor array disabled.

Another Ci'in and three more Kwia from the other truck joined us, mounting up and putting on their helmets. We tested the lights attached above our visors, LEDs flashed at each tap. I ran my hands over my vest, then my weapons, for the fifth time, then started up my bike.

With night-vision, Casey and I led the way up the mountain trail. It was rough going in the dark, but we finally reached the transection point. We'd wait here until we knew it was safe to go on. I gave critters and snakes a warning before we collapsed under a rock outcropping.

Casey waited until I was settled in. Two Kwia stood guard above us. I was the first to unfasten my bullet-proof vest, rubbing at my ribs and taking a refreshing drink. The other Ci'in did the same, dabbing her neck with water. It might still be a cool desert night, but under the gear we were sweating.

Chucky joined us. "Let's take another look at the plan."

With a grunt, Casey smoothed out the sand in front of us. I drew the wash from memory, leading up to the base of the plateau. Topography had shown us where the water cut down into the rocks, the current foliage and outcroppings would keep us from being sighted visually. Our Kwia would run an advance team. I'd bring up the rear.

We weren't too far from our target, and right now the other teams were settling into their attack positions, but we had to wait for Joey's signal. We'd selected three points of attack.

One had been a place not far from where Lutz and I took our video. From there teams could rappel down onto the plateau. Another team would drop from the other side of the plateau, above the area they stored the vehicles. We'd come up from through the wash and block that exit route.

The Maxa'xak would try to escape. It's what they did since the first time we came after them. It was their only way to survive with their weak numbers. Had they had more time before we discovered their existence, they might have succeeded in breeding a stronger species.

If they'd escaped undetected, they might have succeeded in finding an adaptable species for procreation, but we refused to allow their infestation. We would either pin this Maxa'xak down or they'd drive him straight into my arms. Then it was my job to immobilize him so he could be destroyed.

This was the plan. Everyone agreed, except Casey. I understood his quiet objections. I'd seen many battles and people died. Despite pledging my Spirit to him, I could die. But I was a U.S. Marine and the Ci'in, and my pledges to both made me focus completely on the plan.

I leaned against him, reaching into my pocket and removing the quartz Yazzie had given me. I slipped it into his hand. "Hang onto this to protect your Spirit. It's a symbol for the Earth Element."

"I'd rather it protect you."

"For me." I dropped my head to his chest and he gripped his hand around mine, around the stone. I managed to drift off, listening to desert crickets and Casey's heartbeat.

A Gambel's quail warned us of imminent dawn, singing as the sky just started to lighten. Startled quiet by the chirping of my phone. "The sensors are down."

I struggled up and Casey pulled the vest tight around me, securing it as his lips brushed my forehead ever so slightly. I couldn't give him more and he knew it. He patted the shoulder pocket above his heart. I could see the lump the stone created.

Mounted up, we ran our bikes up the wash, no longer worried about tripping alarms. Taking a sharp bend north, we heard gunfire. Ahead Chucky waved at us. "This way!" I followed, as he was team leader now. I had one job and their job was to make sure I got to the target to complete it.

Around another bend Chucky moved ahead of us, hunched down on his bike, following the brush that lined the wash. I started after him, but an echo sounded and puff of sand made me skid to a stop, staying low under the rock ledge. The rest of my team hunkered down too. Another shot twinged by me, but this time I was watching the angle.

I activated my mic. "Chucky, we're pinned down. Right side of the wash about 40 degrees. One shooter."

"On it." Of course he was.

Still, my hand molded around the grip of my Sig. The feel of the weapon made me more confident, though it wasn't the weapon I'd need when I stood in front of the Maxa'xak.

Casey got into the niche next to me. "Are they trying to clear their escape route?"

"Probably, but he'll try to protect his oldest offspring, letting the younger zombies do the fighting. I only know of the one near maturity, but there could be more." I bobbed up and let go several rounds at our enemy, dodging down as they returned fire. It earned a glare from Casey. "Got to keep them looking at us."

"Then we'll do it. We have to get you to the plateau, not shot down here." He opened up half a clip on them and my father took a turn keeping the enemy distracted. I kept my head down, as ordered. I listening to an endless crescendo of weapons fire, until a large explosion rolled gravel down on top of us.

Casey quickly used his arms to cover me. "What the hell was that?"

"The reason they called us Thunderbirds." My father grinned and returned to his bike. "We can move on now."

Casey dashed to his. "Hey, where's our other Ci'in... Miri-nay?"

I looked back at our group, then heard a brief scream from up the side of the mountain. "Doing her job. Let's go!" I spun my tires, taking the steep slope of the wash. One more bend and we'd be at the access point to the plateau.

We made the turn and ran the bikes up part way, before ditching them to take the alluvial ramp by foot.

"Coming up the other side." Chucky's voice echoed in my ear.

"How many were there?"

Another scream answered that question. "Just the two. Miri-nay will meet us on the plateau when she's done."

"Check." I dashed up the ramp, knowing he'd provide coverage from his position.

Casey stumbled at the high-pitched screams, too high pitched to be human. "What is that? Do they need more help?"

"No, Miri is extracting the larvae from their hosts."

"I thought you said these men were already dead, that what we're doing…"

"They are dead, but the larvae still control the bodies. That's the larvae as she untangles them from the host." I hesitated just a step. "She's killing them before they rip themselves loose and try to make it back to the Maxa'xak, or find another host."

"How would they be introduced to… no, don't answer that."

CHAPTER 31

Casey stood up to give a quick survey of the ramp. Rifle on his shoulder as he did the swing down one mountain face and up the other. "Looks clear."

We were near the top of the alluvial slide they used as a ramp to access the plateau. It was packed down tight enough to handle off-road tires. "Stay against the wall." We kept our backs to the cliff. The gravel here was looser, making the climb tough. We had one last stretch to finish, then we'd be in the battle raging above us.

With another breath, I was ready to rush the last few meters. I had only taken two steps when my skin shivered violently. "Everyone down!" I pulled Casey against the wall as an SUV came off the plateau, hitting the gravel. It slid, the tail end bashing boulders on the other side of the cliff. I switched my Sig to automatic and started firing as it slid towards us. The rest of my party opened fire too.

Tires went out, but that didn't stop them. "Chucky, you in position to hit it?"

"Got it, Sis." Standing up from across the ramp, Chucky pulled a grenade launcher onto his shoulder. "Take cover!"

Cover was hunkering down as close to the wall as possible. Chucky fired on the truck. Casey mashed me against the cliff wall as the grenade hit. I knew this weapon. The grenade would attach itself to the truck and explode. "Shit!"

The truck was lifted off the ground, but rolled in our direction. I cast out an arm. Instinct and training combined to release a blast of energy. A wall of light spread over us, creating a barrier, a force field strong enough to deflect the SUV.

It flipped again, then did a full tumble down the ramp in such a violent bouncing way that it guaranteed no one could survive, seatbelts or not.

I dropped the field, looking up at Chucky across the ramp. "Make sure they're purged."

He ducked off the rock and a moment later two Kwia and Miri were on the SUV, now upside down at the bottom of the cliff. One of the Kwia discharged a sonic disrupter inside the vehicle. Anything possibly alive inside would be dead now, except the larvae.

The men pulled out four bodies, twisted, bloody and broken. The Ci'in knelt down on the chest of the first, cut open the man's throat and thrust a hand down into the incision.

"OH! Really?" Casey looked away.

"That's how it's done." I watched for a second as she started to glow. She focused her energy down into the dead man and in a moment the body started to convulse.

Casey didn't want to watch, but like most humans, couldn't stop himself. He let out a gasp as the woman started pulling. With a jerk she rose up, thrusting a bloody squirming snake-like creature into the air. A Kwia took it from her, threw it to the ground and shoved a white-bladed knife into it.

A sickening scream echoed up to us.

"That thing is in all the… zombies?" Casey skidded on loose gravel, my father shoving him back upright.

"Yeah. Now we have to go. They were only the first attempt. I don't want to be crushed by the second."

My father pushed past both of us. Casey brought up the rear. With a wave from my father, that the way was clear, I reached the top of the ramp, peeking over the edge. Casey popped his head up next to mine, seeing the carnage of the surprise attack on the encampment. Bodies were strewn over the plateau.

The helicopter had been hit. The blades were twisted beyond use and it lay on its side in the center of camp. One of vehicles along the opposing cliff wall was on its side. There was a barrage of weapon fire between our people and mercenaries inside the larger metal building.

I pointed to the smaller building. "That's the mine entrance."

"Looks like a stand-off at the moment."

"Only a moment." I jerked my head up at the cliff over the vehicles. From above I saw ropes dropping down the wall, then Kwia sliding down. Whoever was in the building couldn't see them from their angle.

"They can't destroy all the vehicles. We might need them to get the hostages out."

"Least of our concerns, big picture here, my love." I added the last as I felt him tense next to me. I was almost completely Din'ah right now. "Consider the tens of thousands more lives lost if we fail."

"Right now they're big bulletproof rocks. Just what we need to break the standoff." Chucky made us all jump, slipping up behind us unheard. Sure enough the first Kwia down the rope got into a vehicle and started it up, moving it out of line. Several more vehicles followed, creating a line across the plateau. Kwia warriors ran up beside the SUVs as they slowly crept closer to the buildings. Several climbed inside, dropping the windows enough for their weapons.

One SUV sped out of the lineup, swinging around the smashed helicopter and skidding to a stop right at the top of the ramp. We ducked the spray of gravel. I had my Sig pointed into the SUV as the back passenger door opened. "You need a ride, Princess?"

"Frankie!" I rolled my eyes. "We have coms." I scrambled up the ledge. "I nearly opened fire."

"Me too!" Casey pushed me up and into the SUV. My father piled into the front seat.

"Hey, thought you'd prefer a layer of bulletproof glass over sticking your heads up over the rocks."

"I do." I tossed myself against the opposite door, watching as the other SUVs carried our people closer and closer to the buildings. Daniel and his group were in the forward position now. He had a sonic charger. One per vehicle and all aimed at the largest building.

When they opened fire, the metal siding crumpled and shredded like aluminum foil. Daniel strolled out from behind his vehicle and towards the smaller building, knelt and let go another blast. The wood and metal shack collapsed. Whatever was in there would take a while to crawl out.

Time we needed.

With return fire quelled, a group of Kwia warriors stormed the remains of the larger structure, warily. The first two went in. There were a series of clicks on my earpiece and the rest of the team followed. A few minutes later they came out, rushing across the plateau to the nearest vehicle, six women clung to their rescuers, crying, even as they were tossed into the backs of the SUVs.

"There's some of our hostages." I thrust open the door to the SUV, climbing out. Other Ci'in started across the plateau, stopping at each body to perform extractions. Their eerie glow preceded screams that echoed against the walls.

Casey tried not to look as he took a defensive position on my right. "What about the women? You're not checking them."

"Completely incompatible hosts. He uses them as slave labor." A man in front of us started to push up off the ground. I was a step closer than my Kwia. I shoved the man down with my boot and dropped a single shot into the back of his skull. I stepped over the body, leaving the extraction for another Ci'in.

Casey hesitated by the body and I felt Beth squirm inside my brain. "Zombie. You've got to remember that."

Casey stepped around the body, as if the larvae might come after him. "They don't like women?"

"Nope." The combination of my ancient and modern knowledge pulled together an explanation. "Think of it as an extreme case of Hostile Womb Syndrome. When a woman gets pregnant, her body naturally starts producing antibodies to kill the invader, until it recognizes it as a fetus. For some reason a larva triggers this same syndrome, but HWS doesn't stop until it kills the larva. At the same time killing the host. Happens every time."

I stopped by another body. "In men's bodies the larvae only have to overcome the normal immune system." I gave this body an extra bullet too.

"So even if the zombie looks dead, kill it again." The Kwia fired into the next body we passed. "Unless a Ci'in has done her thing."

"This is insane."

Casey sounded horrified, but I didn't give in to Beth's desire to comfort him. "If you can't handle it, return to the SUV, because it's going to get a lot uglier. These were only the younger minions. We'll encounter the older ones when we get into the mine." I spared him a bit of sympathy. "This is our war, not yours."

"Maybe, but it's my planet, my people." Casey firmed up his resolve, pulling his shoulders back. "Even if you got a thousand Ci'inkwia backing you up, you're not facing this without me."

CHAPTER 32

Casey kept whatever other objections he had to himself as we made our way to the mine entrance. Chucky joined me at the edge of the demolished building. He tapped at his ear piece. "Daniel confirms the extractions we're making are all less than fifty years old. Maxa'xak must have his older offspring down there with him."

I could see the shaft where it entered the mountain. "Escape possibilities?"

"Joey's rerouted the scanner arrays and they're watching for any movement. Says it was all pretty sophisticated."

"Maybe, but doubt there's an escape tunnel." Frankie joined us. "I went on a lot of the mine inspections. Those old miners were paranoid. It's easier to hide one entrance than two."

My father nodded. "It's hard to dig in this area. Best he could have done, without massive equipment, was shore up the old mine." He looked back to the alluvial ramp. "He'd have to dispose of the debris, which might have contributed to the ramp, but any other piles would have drawn attention."

Daniel joined us, letting his sonic charger slip back between his shoulders. "Got a few answers from the women. There's cells carved into the tunnel walls, where they're holding the rest of their people. They don't know what else is beyond those points, but they know the Maxa'xak lives down there. You ready?"

All eyes turned to me. "As I'll ever be." I turned back to the killing field, shutting my ears to the screams. "We have innocents down there. If we can get them out, we need to try. If we run into any that have been newly infested, we should leave them for last. Concentrate on the ones that can fight back."

"We have teams arranged for this phase." My father stepped close to me, taking my hands. "You concentrate on the task in front of you and be careful. You haven't had as much time as we did to adapt to what we are and our mission here. Listen to your brothers." He leaned down and gave me a kiss on my cheek. "Listen to yourself. You are very much loved and we want you to come back from this."

"I love you too, Papa." I embraced him. It wasn't often he displayed emotions and they cut through the rigidness of my Spirit side, touching my heart. Him reaching out, at this moment, made what was about to happen all the more serious. "I'll listen to them."

I got another kiss on the cheek, before he slipped out of the circle. Everyone else was quiet, giving me a moment of quiet so I could recompose myself. Even Frankie was subdued. Casey stroked my back, easing off as Din'ah finally came back to the surface.

Another breath and she was back. "Get the tunnel crew together. We head down now."

Daniel and Chucky split out. I heard their orders over our com. A group of Kwia started clearing the tunnel entrance, under the cover of Frankie and several more Kwia. I waited to the side, reloading my Sig.

No one fired up on us. Daniel's charge had taken out two mercenaries near the entrance. Their bodies were dragged out and the larvae extracted. Frankie took his team and advanced into the tunnel ahead of us.

I waited a few minutes with my group. "Remember, we check every nook and cranny. No one leaves without being checked twice."

Some of the Ci'in in this group were well-blooded from extractions. "Team one, your Ci'in needs recovery time. You'll remain on the surface and rest. Team two, you'll do the final check of anyone leaving the mine. Make sure no one comes up without an escort. Prep victims for relocation and rotate down as we need replacements. Team three, you are all fresh, so you come with me now." They all nodded.

I gave everyone one last long look. "Then let's go." I led them into the dark. "You see anything that slithers, kill it."

Hands went to white-bladed knives. More than ritual. Made from the materials of the Maxa'xak escape ship. Strong enough to bring them light years from our home. Strong enough to kill the Maxa'xak. Stepping into the dark, I let my hand slide over the hilt of my knife too.

Only a few yards down the steep sloped shaft, our advance team reached a bend. They tossed phosphorescent light tubes around the corner before daring the turn. We followed, lining the walls with brighter light blocks.

Enough light to make sure there weren't any crevices or nooks where something could hide.

Searching involved more than sight. Ci'in had different abilities than Kwia. We could sense the presence of the Maxa'xak and their offspring. The Maxa'xak had inhabited this tunnel long enough its foul energy permeated the walls, antagonizing our energy, giving us all a soft glow of warning.

Looking at my hands, I knew it was a good thing my Rising came so late. If I'd lit up on our first encounter with these people, we'd have been shot right there.

Thinking of Lutz got him glimmering next to me, earning expletives from the team.

Chucky turned around to see what was wrong, leveling his weapon. "Who's this?"

"This is Sgt. Brandon Lutz, my partner."

"Her dead partner." Casey elaborated.

"Ouch, dude! Don't you think that's a bit insensitive?"

"Really?" Chucky glared at Lutz. "How long has he been here?"

Lutz snickered wickedly. "Dude, I've been hanging around all night, waiting for you people to get here." He wrapped an arm around my shoulder. "Now maybe I can lend a hand."

"Like what? Can you go see what the Maxa'xak is doing?"

"No, he can't." Casey and I both answered at the same time, earning Casey a glare for keeping Lutz secret.

"Ease up, bro. I can go a little ways ahead, all within the life-force energies thing."

"Well, that could be helpful. Get up there, soldier."

"Yes, ma'am." He said it with a wink and took off at a trot, in full view this time.

I got curses in my headset from Frankie, and laughter from Casey. I gave him the eye now. "Maybe I should have sent you to do introductions.

"Like you didn't do that to him on purpose." Chucky sniped as he took the wall across from me.

I tapped my com. "He wants to help. Make sure we don't walk into a trap." Almost as soon as I said it, a stop order came through our headset. I listened to part of a message before Lutz reappeared.

"Take cover! Percussion grenade."

I stuck my fingers in my ears, everyone else quick to do the same, dropping down and facing the wall. An explosion sent a cloud of dust rolling up to us. We barely waited for it to clear before we were moving, weapons ready as we heard shots fired.

Chucky pushed me back into Casey as we reached our advance team. The shooting had stopped and they had dropped to defensive positions, weapons pointed into the darkness just beyond a new glow stick.

Four men lay dead against the walls. Lutz reappeared. "That cleared the next bend. You can see what's in the rooms now."

Frankie stood up. "Thanks, sergeant." I got a sideways growl from him. "Anymore friends you want to introduce?"

"Hey, you almost walked into them." Lutz came to my defense.

"Rooms?" I raised my voice over them both, shaking loose of Casey.

Frankie backed down and took his team, now including Lutz ahead, then gave us an all clear. We turned the corner to find a widened section of the tunnel, with metal doors cut into the walls.

Not human height, but half as high. Their color was the same as the rock and they had a coating of dust from the explosion.

Lutz reappeared. "There's more as we go deeper, but I can only go so far ahead of you. Unless someone I know joins the advance team." Lutz pointed to Casey. "I need energy to feed off of."

"Will do."

"NO!" I answered at the same time Casey agreed. I couldn't let Beth out, but she was alarmed, as was I. "You know Frankie now. Use his energy."

"It has to be someone I knew when I was alive." Lutz shrugged. "Manifesting 201."

"Not funny. I'm not letting you get yourself shot. You're not even supposed to be here."

"As your husband, I am." Casey checked his weapon, then his vest. "Come on." He jerked his head Lutz. "Let's expand your territory."

Before I could keep arguing, they moved around Chucky, who squinted at me.

"Shut up." I glared back, knowing he was about to admonish me for being too human. It wasn't the first time either. How frequently had the fates put us into the same family? Fates being the Great Mother. She had more of a sense of humor than the Great Father who was off somewhere throwing random energies together to see what happened.

We hunkered down as Lutz brought Casey's reports. A few more percussion grenades went off. They cleared the tunnel a hundred feet deeper and were ready to hold the tunnel.

I turned to the first door.

CHAPTER

33

I ran my hands over the door, but felt no active bad Spirits on the other side. I stood back to let several Kwia surrounded the door. Two stood ready with weapons cocked, the third opened the door from behind and tossed in a light stick. There was the sound of scurrying, then stillness.

“Come out, now. Hands on your heads.” Chucky shouted. Nothing happened.

“In Spanish.” I didn’t hold back the sarcasm.

Chucky repeated himself slowly and hands poked out of the hole, then a man’s face. He did as he was told, crawling through the low door on his knees, hands on his head. A woman crawled out after him on all fours, her eyes wide as she blinked and looked around at us. She started rattling off pleas in Spanish, crying.

"Shhh. We're here to get you out." I didn't wait for my warriors to figure out what to say, Spanish being one of the many languages I knew. I reached a hand out to her, but first let it graze over the man's upraised arm. No glow. "Come on."

She avoided my hand, dropping her face to dirt floor, praying as tears came faster. She was invoking St. Zavala. Believing I was her, the other Ci'in being my angels. She prayed that I save their lives and souls. I stepped back. *Why wouldn't she think that? We were glowing.*

"Get up and go with one of these soldiers. They'll get you to safety." I rattled it off firmly, stepping out of their way.

The man managed to get to his feet. Hands still on his head, letting them down slowly to help the woman up. Still nothing to show he was infested as he passed by me and a Ci'in took his arm. She gave me a nod to confirm he was clean.

They stumbled, the woman still crying. As I turned around, Chucky was kneeling down to peer inside the room. "Damn!" He covered his face, backing away. "Fucking animals."

I looked into the cell, glowing green with the light stick. It was barely more than a hole in the wall, a little longer than wide, maybe six-by-eight. A bucket was against one wall, two more on the other wall. I didn't have to go inside to know one was a toilet. I could smell it. "They had no choice."

"I wasn't talking about them." Chucky headed for the next cell door.

I couldn't blame him for his disgust, but I knew it was only going to get worse.

Three more cells released the same grateful, desperate hostages. We had the cycling pattern down as we reached the next section of tunnel and sets of doors. I leaned against the wall behind the door, then jumped back. I'd started to glow hotter. "Bingo!"

The Kwia at the door backed away. "The stench. Something in there is dead."

"It isn't the larva." I looked at the cells we'd already passed. In ten thousand years we still didn't know everything about the infestation process. We didn't want to and only learned what we did from those hostages rescued before their turn came.

It was brutal. The victim became nothing more than a wild animal. A wild animal in such pain that its only reaction is to kill. This was the stage where they usually died, but this one hadn't. He was strong enough to make my skin crawl.

I swung my rifle around and rapped on the cell door. Something inside threw itself against the door in response, the screeching inhuman. "Give me a glow stick."

One plopped into my hand and with some twisting, I tore off the end, using the gel to mark the door as I'd seen in dozens of plague disaster movies, only with a 'Z' for zombie. "No one needs to see what's inside these cells until we have to."

Everyone agreed.

Two more cells yielded uninfected hostages, the third gave me a bad vibe, but a woman's voice answered the rap. She pleaded for help, that her husband was sick. I gave the Kwia a nod to open the door and she spilled out, kneeling on the ground, her clothes torn until almost nonexistent.

Deep scratches ran down her arms and legs, and across one cheek. She rattled off words, pointing inside the cell.

"We'll take care of him." I nodded to the team to take her out of the cave. They pulled her off the ground, carrying her weak body away. She kept begging us to help her husband. I couldn't tell her he was beyond help. I certainly couldn't let her see what would happen to him.

A glow stick was tossed into the hole. Against the back wall was the man. I could see why her clothes were nothing but rags. She used them to make restraints, tying his arms and legs. Smart woman. From the way he was thrashing around and gnashing his teeth, I doubt she'd still be alive to beg for his salvation.

When I got the message she was in the hands of triage, I gave Chucky a nod. He locked the door, marking it. I moved on. "How many of these cells are there?"

"Eleven more." Lutz appeared ahead of me, walking backwards. "The guy we ran into that first day is in the group heading down. He doesn't look too good, but I don't see any wounds. He's stumbling and two others are carrying him. I think that thing is happening to him."

"Maturity? Shit!" I turned back to Chucky. "I don't have time for this. Lutz says we got a new Maxa'xak emerging."

"Got it." He spun back. "Split up. If you speak Spanish, stay here to evacuate the victims. If you get a live response, open it. Get a glow and no human, mark it." He waved his arm as he turned towards me. "Everyone else with us."

Lutz disappeared, returning to our advance team. Another round of explosions sounded, screams, then clearance to move on. We kept running into assailants, sacrifices meant to slow us down.

They had no concern for their own survival, only gaining time for the new offspring to emerge and escape. If it chewed itself free before we got to it, it would be small enough to slip into the cracks and crevices of this mountain, this aquafer. It could evade us for ages.

"Hold up. They set explosives to cave in the tunnel."

Chuck jerked and swung away from Lutz' sudden materialization, stomping his feet as he pointed his M9 at the ceiling. "Damn it! Announce yourself before popping up like that. My trigger finger is jumpy enough."

"Sorry, dude." Lutz grinned. "You can shoot me if it'll make you feel better."

"Sarcasm from the dead guy. Cute."

I turned to the group. "Bombs… anyone?"

"Did you see the final hook up?" A Ci'in stepped out of the team.

"Yeah. Electronic trigger. Watched them wire it." Lutz shrugged. "I took training classes for IEDs. I can't touch it, but I can talk."

"That much is clear." Chucky snarked at him.

"Man, I wish I was still alive. You seem like a hoot to hassle." Lutz grinned as Chucky pointed his gun at him. "Casey's going to have to be close enough for me to feed."

"Please! Don't phrase it like that. It's bad enough we got zombies, I don't need a vampire ghost image in my head too."

"Okay, borrow from." Lutz rolled his eyes and waved at the volunteer. "Come on, unless you're afraid of ghosts too, like Chucky here."

“I’m not afraid of ghosts!” Chucky fumed and glared at me. “Figures your friends are just like you.”

“Yeah, she rubbed off on me.”

“Both of you. Mission, zombies, a pissed off Xak and its baby…”

Our volunteer Ci’in eased between us. “I got a mini-kit on me. She tapped a tool belt on her hip, giving Lutz a grin. “I don’t mind mouthy ghosts. Had a few in my time. You humans like to hang on to those you left behind.”

“Only until I have to go.” Lutz stepped aside and gave her a chivalrous bow. “This way, my dear.”

She trotted away with him just like he was a normal guy flirting with her. We followed behind as she left us a trail of light cubes. We reached half of the advance team, set up to stop us from going deeper. Bomb perimeter.

“How much further?” I knelt down next to the team lead.

“About a hundred feet. Your guy indicated it was just enough explosives to seal off the section, not cave in the whole mine.”

“Good to know. Any word from our tech?”

“No, she and the rest of the team left their com-sets. Electronic trigger and all.”

“Great, so we know absolutely nothing.” Chucky was across from me.

“Not ideal, I agree, but necessary. Once we get past this trap we need to get Lutz back on their position, so we know what’s happening. One second too late and no one goes home.” It was a bittersweet goal, eons old, but one I wanted to fulfill for us all.

I waited a few more minutes, but waiting with no word was more than I could bear. In two steps I slipped past the warriors prone with their rifles. Chucky cursed out loud, coming after me. “Seriously, Sis, I don’t know where this streak came from.”

“Kettle, pot. You’re just as bad, and it ain’t our first round, brother.” I pointed from him to myself as I slid along the wall at a crouch until I came up behind Casey.

He looked up at me as I knelt behind him. “Can you two stop sniping at each other?”

CHAPTER

34

Casey shut us up for a few minutes, but I was feeling the Maxa'xak, and the urgency. Snipping at Chucky took the edge off, but I resisted. It took another five minutes before we heard a little 'yip' from up ahead. "All clear."

With that, I took off again. Lutz buzzed ahead of us, trying to catch up with the enemy. A few more bends and I didn't need his help to know we were close. My whole body shimmered with energy.

Casey saw it too, grabbing at my arm each time I tried to slip past him. "You wait until we can see what's ahead of us. Last thing we need is you setting off an ambush. We got them cornered, making them all a hundred times more dangerous."

"That's right. Listen to him." Chuck said it firm enough it wasn't just him snarking at his little sister.

"It's hard." The imbalance between the three of us, Ci'in, Kwia and Maxa'xak created a force all of its own, a magnetic draw that sucked me towards it. Drawing me forward to extinguish the bad energy and return the universe to the proper balance. “This is why I’m here.”

The grip on my arm tightened, reminding me Casey had hold of me. It was the same sensation as during my Rising, the rope that bound us, his blood against my skin. It worked against the overwhelming urge to rush into battle. He drew my feet back to the ground.

“Hang onto me a bit longer.”

“As long as I can.” His fingers dug into my arm, restraining my bloodlust for the Maxa’xak.

A few more meters and the advance team dropped to the floor. They started firing into the dark ahead of them. Cubes of light were thrown into the blackness and immediately weapon fire was returned. We all hit the ground.

Level ground. We were either at the bottom of the mine or one of the last levels. That was better than being fired upon from below, but the cavern ahead was off to the left of the tunnel opening, meaning our warriors were shooting around a corner.

I crawled up behind them, waiting for them to open up a barrage so I could stick my head out to get a view of the cavern. A quick image, then back in response to Casey jerking on my leg. I curled around and pulled out another light stick, stabbing it with my knife.

“We need more cubes in there, but this is what I saw.” Using the stick like a pen I drew out the cavern. “There’s another tunnel or cavern there. There’s a debris pile right here.” I blobbed gel to the side of the cavern. “That’s where the shooters are. We need some good throwers.”

Two of the Kwia and Chucky raised hands. "Grenades, percussion and smoke. Then Frankie, take your group to that pile and take out the shooters. From there launch the next assault. Knock them off their feet and give us time to get through." I nodded to the Ci'in. "Hold on extractions, just make sure they can't get up again."

"Got it." Frankie pulled out what he had left of his grenades, as did everyone else, handing them off to our throwers. We moved back while Chucky's team joined the men keeping the enemy on edge. The three men took a moment to prepare themselves, each getting a quick peek between gunfire outbursts, timing their assault.

They opened up another final barrage of bullets at the enemy line. Simultaneously, Chucky and his Kwia stepped into the cavern and started lobbing grenades.

I jerked at the same instant one of our throwers dropped to his knees. Chucky snatched his live grenade, threw it and shoved the wounded Kwia back towards Frankie. As soon as all the grenades were tossed, the team switched, Frankie charging the debris pile.

I met the throwers, who'd picked up their wounded man to drag him to the wall. Chucky let go, swinging his rifle around and following Frankie into the cavern.

The man in my arms slid down the wall. I could hear him gasping and pulled his bullet-proof vest open. He was hit right where the vest opened on the side, probably as he raised his arm to throw a grenade. I ripped open his shirt, forcing him to his side. "I think it hit a lung."

I folded his fingers back over the wound, feeling a ring. He was Bound. Someone was waiting to see him again. "We'll call a team to come and get you. We have to go."

"Go. Go." He tried to wave me away, without losing his grip. We'd been doing this long enough he knew the risks and that we had a higher obligation. I gathered myself and stood up. Someone was already calling for a triage team. For him and for anyone else wounded as we attacked.

The next round of grenades was my signal. I pulled out my knife and the rest of my team followed.

Smoke made it hard to see, but I felt the enemy ahead of us. They were in pain and confused, the grenades did the job intended. I found the pile of rocks, their cover. I hit the first boulder and jumped, seeing five men collapsed on the ground as I came down on the other side. None of them the man who'd stopped us the first day. No Maxa'xak.

No, that energy came from the hole these men were left to protect. My whole body was on fire. Two men conscious enough reached for their weapons. They didn't have time. From above a rain of bullets struck them. Their bodies jerked with each impact, until they were still.

I stepped over the body between me and the next cavern. Before I got another step, I heard a sound, a growl and something metal against stone. Then I was struck from above and knocked to the ground.

It wasn't one of the enemy, no one infested. I rolled and then saw Casey's face. He rolled as well, carrying us both to the back wall of this nook in the rocks. The ricocheting of bullets pinged above and around us.

"You don't walk into a hole like that!" Casey snapped at me, trying to look over his shoulder, but we were barely covered by the boulder we'd landed behind. "Stop acting like you're iron-clad. Part of you is still human and I don't want to lose you."

"Sorry!" I could see what was going on. My team were still behind the barricade, firing into the cavern I was so willing to walk into. "Cover!" I reached for my ears as I saw a grenade fly through the air towards the black cavern. A light cube went with it.

"Damn." Casey got his hands to his head, but winced.

The explosion and the deep vibrating thump was deafening. This close it sucked the breath out of us. I gasped to get it back as I pushed Casey off me. Only then I saw blood spreading down his sleeve and his shoulder looked wrong. "Damn it!"

My Beth side struggled to help him, but I couldn't. Over the rock came the rest of my team. Ci'in going for the downed enemy to finish off their larvae. Chuck appeared and saw Casey was shot. He grabbed two Kwia. "Take him back to the tunnel, now!"

My hand was slow letting go. Chucky jerked me to my feet. "Get yourself under control. We got seconds before they start shooting again."

Casey let out a teeth-grit groan as one Kwia grabbed his feet, the other the straps of his vest and lifted him up. They took off, back around the rocks and towards the tunnel.

Chucky shook me again. It was all I needed. I focused on the two larger prey waiting inside. Waiting for me.

CHAPTER

35

I took a deep breath. Two strong Ci'in on either side of me, a row of Kwia in front, we entered the dark chamber. The zombie soldier who'd fired on us lay at the entrance, body riddled by bullets. Light cubes flashed to life ahead of us, opening us to a scene straight out of some dark fantasy.

Coiled at the back of the cave was the Maxa'xak, hissing and spitting in rage. The truncated arms were curled up close to its body, but the claws clacked loud. The slimy flesh glowed, just as we Ci'in, but a sickly color under the light of the cubes. His eyes blazed like fire, glaring at me.

"This will end, here!" I spread out my arms, releasing my full Ci'in, shouting in the language we'd preserved from our birth.

"A chosen Ci'in." It raised its head and hissed, but the sound was pleasure. "It has been long since I have feasted on the blood of one so high."

“Do not salivate for her flesh yet. She isn’t alone.” From behind us came Daniel’s voice. He stepped up behind me, Frankie with him, Chucky among the Kwia in front me.

The pleasure disappeared in the Maxa’xak’s hissing. In a flash that huge head lunged for me, but I was prepared. My Ci’in were prepared, their hands each grasping my shoulders as I thrust a hand outward.

Fed by their energy, a bright burning light flashed in the face of the beast and it let out a scream. The Kwia with us opened fire as it thrashed to clear the mass of energy clinging around its head. With the Maxa’xak’s power disrupted, our bullets penetrated the protective shield wrapped around its hide like a second skin.

It screamed and I thrust another bolt into his face, my power boosted as two more Ci’in joined us. My brothers kept pace as I moved forward, their weapons ready to strike at the Maxa’xak.

Bullets bombarded our foe, wounding it, making it writhe and try to draw away. We would wear it down until my brothers could strike with their knives.

Focused on him, I barely saw the figure lunge at me from the shadows. I cast out my other hand, but felt a blade strike down into my forearm. The pain was enough to make me waver in the force I used against the Maxa’xak. It struck out at the nearest Kwia. Our man screamed as the huge mouth closed around him, fangs sinking deep.

Frankie pushed the assailant off me and I was able to throw another ball of fire at the beast, blinding it for an instant. It recoiled and everyone started shooting again. There was no regard for our brother. He no longer screamed and we had to assume he was dead.

I turned to the man who'd attacked me. He crouched on the ground like an animal, ready to pounce. It was the Smirker, his eyes wild, his upper body twisting strangely. The mature Maxa'xak was trying to break free. "Hold our ancient friend. I have to finish this task first."

The Maxa'xak had probably tried to hide his offspring, distract us for as long as it needed for the mature monster to tear itself free of the host. But madness was impossible to control, even for a few more minutes.

I ran towards the man, knife drawn. He stumbled at my attack, falling backwards as I landed on him. My hand closed around his throat. "It is time to set your host free. Let me help you."

My own blood drained down onto his flesh. He screamed as the energy in my body burned him. He screamed with the voice of the monster inside him. I could feel it alive beneath the flesh. Down inside his open mouth the tissues bulged, already starting to bleed as the monster clawed to escape.

So close to escape. So close to the pool of water casting strange shimmers around the cavern. An underground well fed by the water table. *If it broke free and got into that well...* With a thrust, I shoved my white-bladed knife straight down into his throat, slicing him open.

The new Maxa'xak coiled free, lashing fangs at me. His parent let out an eerie shriek and instead of attacking me further, the infant lunged for the water. I was just as fast chasing it, not thinking of the parent starting to regain control again.

Before I could reach it another white-bladed knife buried itself in the middle of the new Maxa'xak. Frankie pinned it to the ground and with a smooth swipe, sliced it in half the long way.

Its scream was nothing compared to the one our giant enemy let loose. "Noooooo!" A half-blinded beast turned itself on him. "You will die."

I lunged too, pushing Frankie out of the way. I rolled with him, but one of those fangs grazed the back of my thigh. One more roll let me see it rising to strike again, at me. I thrust out both hands.

Pure light radiated from me, slowing time, but not my actions. My hands closed around the long fangs just inches before they skewered me. I clung to them, sending all my energy beyond, into the eyes of the beast still bearing down on me.

The weight of the beast pressed down upon my arms as my power held it. The body shook, but his head was frozen above me. His eyes, black as the tunnel had been when we entered. Deadly, soulless eyes. Eyes of a madness no creature should carry.

This creature lacked the duality to counter insanity. It wanted to be alive, to be whole, to be free from the burning hunger, but there was no balance. There could never be balance.

I stared into those hateful eyes and some distant part of me felt a sliver of sympathy. Deep inside I could sense our siblings, trapped in the nightmare of their mistake. How they suffered. "You are the last. Your pain is done. We will give you a final rest."

In my grip his defensive shield couldn't sustain itself. My brothers attacked, their knives able to penetrate deeper than the bullets they'd used to distract the beast. Their slashes threw black blood as they cut down through thick flesh. Frankie jumped onto the spine of the Maxa'xak, taking aim with his dagger, using both hands as he plunged it in, drawing it down to expose the vertebrae.

"Hurry!" My grip on the fangs started to slip from its saliva and my blood, barbs along the back of each fang cut into my fingers.

Frankie's eyes met mine. "Hold on another minute, Princess." His tone wasn't harsh, but pleading with me. He thrust his blade down between the vertebrae. Twisting, leaning his entire weight onto his knife. "Someone help her!"

I'd tried to ignore the numbness spreading up my leg and down my arms. Poison in those fangs was entering my bloodstream, but I couldn't release my control. I had to keep hold of this monster until my brothers could kill it. I had to hold on.

A burst of energy flowed through me as the four Ci'in crowded around me, touching me with one hand, the Maxa'xak with their other hands. Pushing against the massive dying weight. I pulled on what they offered me, sending it up into this beast, burning at its brain as my brothers tried to kill it.

I had to keep it paralyzed, unable to fight back, even if it killed me. It had to die before I did. I let all the power of my Ci'in flow outward, but we were in a death grip. I could feel its fangs sinking into me. I felt my pain, and its anguish as Daniel and Chucky ripped the wounds open wider to help Frankie sever the central nervous system.

I wanted to scream. *One more minute...* More hands pressed upwards on its head. They pushed, their hands burning into the skin of the Maxa'xak as the fangs punctured my abdomen. I felt them rip upwards as the massive head was pushed away from me.

He was screaming in my head and all I could do was keep promising it a freedom he didn't want. "It's almost done. You'll be returned to the elements you rose from. Your Spirit released from the agony. Let it happen. Let go."

It screamed louder as Frankie's knife struck home. "That's it!" I thought I yelled it out loud, but I couldn't hear my own voice. The beast trembled and the crazy in those eyes started to fade. "You will be at peace now." I spoke into those eyes, my mind linked to his.

"You… will go… with me." It thrashed one last time, tossing Frankie from its back.

Despite the strength and energy of the Ci'in helping me, one fang cut across my abdomen again as the Maxa'xak went into death throes. The massive head swung away, knocking the Ci'in down. Someone grabbed me, pulling me back. I felt the spines on the back of the fangs tearing at my hands. It should have hurt, but strangely it didn't.

"Din'ah!"

I heard my name screamed and the pressure of hands on my body, turning me over. Frankie knelt over me. "Din'ah, how bad are you hurt?"

I couldn't answer. Two Ci'in started ripping open my vest, then my shirt. Another was twisting my hip. "Got two laceration across her stomach, another down her leg. She must have toxins in her blood."

"And her hands. Real deep. Damn! We need a full medical team and every free Ci'in." Frankie gripped my face, even though his hands were covered with the blood of the Maxa'xak. "Look at me, Princess. You have to hang on. Hear me? HANG ON!"

I couldn't move, only stare up at him. He sounded so scared. None of the anger I was used to hearing from him.

"Din'ah!" Daniel leaned down close to me too, partly blocking out my vision of Frankie. "We're not going to let you die."

I settled my eyes on his. I couldn't speak, but there was one image in my head now. I only wanted one thing, one person now. I couldn't say it, but Daniel nodded.

CHAPTER
36

The pain was gone and in its place was nothing but light. Breathing in sent tingles through my entire body. Life, my real life. I was a creature of light, of energy, of infinity. I lived among the stars. They gave me life and I shared it with them. It flowed into me now. Pure light, wiping away the pain, the agony.

Ten thousand years was nothing, except for living it in mortal bodies. So many lives. So many people, so many deaths. These humans had no idea how little they knew of the universe. Their lives were short, even though lived over and over again. But as a people, they could only do this singularly. Such a lonely existence. It made my heart ache…

Wait. I have no mortal body, no heart. Death has brought me back to my own. So why was there an ache so deep within this consciousness? I felt the light pouring into me, eternal life, but… there was something else. Something heavier. Something clinging to me.

"Have you forgotten already?" Opening my eyes I saw Lutz' Spirit, looking disappointed. "You made a promise." His hand led my eyes to the scene laid out before me.

I looked upon horror and remembered everything. "The battle is over." Bodies were scattered around the cavern, as well as the dead Maxa'xak. "We destroyed all of them. Our duty is done. The universe was in balance again. We can go home. Why do I feel this pain?"

"Because you're forgetting two others you made a promise to." Lutz shook his head, drifting towards the cluster of people below.

The light was unmistakable. Ci'in circled together, combining their Spirits. I moved closer and saw their combined light flowing into my wounded mortal body. The Maxa'xak had torn long poisoned gashes across her body. She was dying. I started to call out to them to let her go, but I couldn't.

Crumpled next to her was Casey. He was wounded too, but alive. He clung to her arm, refusing to look away from her. His pain for her was greater than his own.

"You promised him. You Bound yourself to him. You can do what I couldn't. You can keep your vow."

"I did promise, but she is weak."

"If you let go she will die." He pointed to Casey. "It might very well kill him too. If not, his pure soul will be damaged."

I stared down at Casey. He was the entity I felt, the sorrow preventing me from leaving. I let myself be Bound to him. His hand tightened on her arm and I felt it. Other Ci'in arrived with medical supplies and started cutting away her clothes, revealing how badly her body was battered.

One leg was flayed open, there was a puncture wound on her right hip and a long gash across her abdomen. The skin blackening where the venom was already killing the flesh. Skin was peeled off her hands where they'd been torn loose from the monster's fangs.

A respirator pushed oxygen into her lungs. The Ci'in sent all their energy into her too, trying to drive off the alien toxins. She fought to live. I could feel how much she wanted to live. She wanted to live for Casey. She loved him with her entire soul. My soul, my Spirit.

"She can't survive without you. You owe her whatever life lays ahead. A few more decades are only a blink of an eye for you. A few more decades are nothing to repay her sacrifice for you. For all the mortal sacrifices given to you."

"I know. I gave my word." I looked at Lutz. "I also promised to release you. Others can do that, but I owe you that respect. I keep my word."

"She is as much you as you are her, but I was just afraid this side might be too tempting." Lutz touched my arm. "Go to them."

"I am Bound." I let myself drift closer to Beth. With one more breath of the pure energy that comprised this universe, I melted down into her. I felt the touch of Casey's hand, the pull of his soul, his heart, the Bounding of my Spirit to his.

Light burned through my eyelids. I tried to turn my face away from it, but my head didn't move.

"She's definitely waking up!"

I didn't recognize the voice and forced my eyes open. A woman in uniform. A Marine uniform with medical emblems on the lapels. *A doctor? We didn't bring the Marines.*

"Capt. Castle, can you hear me?" I tried to answer, but my throat hurt with the slightest thought of it. "Blink twice. You've got a breathing tube in."

I blinked twice, rolling my eyes from side to side. There were other military here, mixed in among the Ci'inkwia. Yazzie popped up next to me. "Thank the Spirits!" She looked genuinely relieved. "We called in the Marines as soon as we realized we were under attack."

"Though it seems you managed without us. We have troops combing the mountains for anyone that might have slipped past your…" She looked around the plateau. "…warriors. Don't know exactly what you people were up to here, but these Coyotes made a mistake interrupting your little pow-wow, Captain."

"It was an honored ceremony!" Yazzie stiffened, looking quite indignant. "The 'Captain' is more than…"

Yazzie stopped as I let out a groan, pain, as well as wariness.

She bowed her head to me, but didn't relent. "There are many tribes and many things YOUR people will never understand. Capt. Castle is a Spirit Woman, but highest among ALL our tribes. She is the Ci'in!" She stood firm against the doctor. "She and those wounded or killed were important to us, including our friend, Sgt. Lutz."

"I'm sorry if I came off as rude. She is important to us too." The doctor sounded sincere. "We will take care of the captain and the wounded." She looked over her shoulder.

"We have more helicopters coming any second to start transporting everyone back to the base."

"Then I will find someone to go with the captain." Yazzie leaned over me. "Your husband will be with you, as well as two medicine women."

"It's a military hospital and there's no need for assistance ..." The doctor pulled out a pocket tablet. "... and I don't see a husband on record for the captain."

"Officer Casey Delgado. One of our ceremonies, before we were attacked. And denying the Ci'in access to her own medicine women is a violation of the captain's religious rights. Do I need to contact the base commander?"

"No…no, no." The doctor shook her head, her eyebrows scrunching together. "We'll figure it out." She tapped at her shoulder, activating the mike on her com. "Alpha flight, the first load is ready to go. Civilian list as follows. One head blunt trauma, one GSW chest. Military injured. One multiple lacerations and burns, one GSW shoulder Two unwounded civilians… medical personnel."

Getting a nod of satisfaction from Yazzie, the doctor focused on me again. "Is this all right with you, captain?" I gave her two blinks, then looked around me again.

This time I could focus better. I saw Casey and jerked my head his way. She looked too. "He's been sedated. Bullet shattered his shoulder. He'll need reconstruction, but we'll know more as soon as we get a proper scan."

My eyes went further, to a string of bodies. Bodies… how were we going to explain this? The doctor followed my gaze and as if reading my mind, glanced at me, then at Yazzie. "The commander is going to have some serious questions."

I blinked again as a helicopters rotors started kicking up dust. The doctor pulled a mask over her face, turning to the other medics. “We need to get everyone out of here now and into detox.” I could see the radioactive biohazard emblem on the face of the mask. She raised a hypo gun. “It’s going to be a bumpy ride, so you’re sleeping through it. See you on the other side.”

CHAPTER

37

There were thousands of questions, taking days to answer, but not until I'd recovered enough to tolerate the long sessions. My 'medicine women' were Ci'in, with me twenty-four hours a day. Via tribal song, they couched me on the constructed story of what happened in the mountains.

They also brought me witness testimony and updates. Members of our party were being unofficially held on the reservation, at the resort. Not a bad imprisonment. The military had argued against it, but the Cocopah guaranteed they'd not let us disappear. Not wanting to get into a pissing match and lose their indefinite land leases, the government capitulated.

I knew about every interrogation and every answer the 'witnesses' gave, including the illegals' testimony. Most of the hostages refused to speak at all. The few who did repeated what they'd been taught by my father. Not that it took a lot of convincing. They knew no one would believe that a giant snake and his army of mercenaries kidnapped them and was using them as incubators. They blamed the deaths of their people on 'Coyotes'.

In his turn, Casey gave testimony. Our 'outing' was supposed to be a dual event, our marriage by ancient tribal customs, before I ascended to the lofty position of "The Ci'in", a secretly elevated Spirit Woman to all the indigenous peoples of the Americas. We'd completed the marriage ceremony the night before ascending the mountain for the second ceremony, where we were attacked.

Individually the stories were believable, but adding in the retaliatory, ritualistic nature of our enemies' deaths, I wasn't surprised they found the collective story incredulous. The investigators argued about the 'eye for an eye' justice and escalated the case. By the time I was fit to testify, it was to an NCIS Inquest.

Since it involved Lutz' death, attacks on citizens of Mexico and the Nation of tribes, I faced my base commander and two generals from Washington D.C.

My scarred hands were folded in front of me as I sat before them. Over the last two days I'd told them the same story from beginning to end, twice already and they picked at it a third time. Now they conferred in tones that white noise prevented me from hearing. But I still knew what they said. Lutz leaned on their table, narrating for me.

All the victims' testimony sided with the actions of my people. We'd rescued them from the murderous hands of Coyotes. To terrify them into compliance, the Coyotes randomly killed someone, in the most horrendous ways possible. Including cutting their throats and ripping them out with their bare hands.

The men asked 'why' over and over again, getting the same answers. They were running an illegal mining operation inside the mountains, but no one could prove it. Before the Marines arrived to 'save us', the tunnel was blown by a small nuclear bomb. Sealing it forever.

Everyone swore it was the last desperate, vengeful act of the Coyotes.

Lutz popped out of existence, reappearing on the edge of my table. "They're at a deadlock." He really liked to carry on conversations when he knew I couldn't answer. His idea of being annoying.

It worked well, but he was useful.

"The general on the left, Gen. Hardass, is on your side. He saw some freaky stuff over in Syria and gets the 'do unto others' angle. And when we came in he was putting on his jacket. He's got the Raider Cross on his right arm."

I gave Hardass a passing glance. I'd worked with his kind. He'd seen lots of battle before he got to the top and understood the truth could be stranger than fiction.

Lutz pointed to the other general. "Gen Marshmallow hasn't seen the front line of anything, but the buffet. He's all 'by the book' and thinks you violated the terms of the oath you swore with all this Ci'in stuff. We need to figure out what he wants to hear to make this go away. So I can say goodbye."

I lowered my head, turning slightly to Lutz. "I'm doing my best."

"Captain!" I jerked my head up as Marshmallow used the microphone to make his voice boom in the hearing room. As if it was necessary. It was a small room "Are we boring you?"

I clenched my teeth, shifting in my seat as I leaned forward. My last pain pill was wearing off. My lips brushed the microphone they'd provided me. "Sir, yes sir."

His mouth popped open. Hardass raised an eyebrow slightly. My commander scrunched up his eyebrows, but didn't say anything.

"I have repeated everything I know. I don't have anything else to add, except that I am… offended. Particularly with your prejudice, sir. My oath to the United States Marine Corps does not negate my religion, any more than it does yours, sir. Nor does it negate the obligation I have to the true native population of this country. Sir."

I turned my arm enough to display the tattoo I shared with Hardass. "I am not a consciousness objector. I have killed to defend our country, our constitution and our people, including the native population you refuse to acknowledge as legitimate. Sir."

"Ewww, go for the jugular by calling him a bigot. Great tactic." Lutz snickered.

There was a stunned moment of recovery as Marshmallow's shock turned to anger. "I am not prejudice, Captain. I am reacting with doubt." He glared at me. "We're supposed to believe that the entire Indian…"

Gen. Hardass cleared his throat, loudly, getting a secondary glare from Marshmallow.

"That the entire Native American…"

"Sir, Earth People." I corrected him, for the tenth time in these hearings. "The National Council of Tribal Affairs has worked for decades to change the derogatory designations to our many tribes. As this is a legal tribunal, please use the correct term. I am of the Earth People. Sir."

He stared at me, looking even more annoyed that I continued to speak back to him. "Captain. You want us to believe that the entire population of… Earth People, picked you as their next great Chin."

I leaned into the microphone again, dropping my voice and speaking slowly, implying in the sheer tone that he was stupid enough I needed to speak slowly. "The Ci'in, sir! As in, The Bishop. The Pope." I got a smirk from Hardass. "I am The Ci'in. And no, it was not the entire population of Earth People, but all the tribal leaders elected to the council. A unanimous vote. Sir." I was maintaining protocol with each statement.

"And they just showed up at your door and dragged you away for this… promotion."

"Yes, sir. They did. The Spirits spoke to the tribal religious leaders, Shaman, as you prefer to call them. The Great Mother told them it was time for a new Ci'in to be appointed. We do not question our Spirits when they speak to us. Sir."

"And these Spirits speak to you now." He said it with such venom, he sounded like the Maxa'xak.

I couldn't help but roll my eyes towards Lutz, who had raised his hand as if volunteering to answer. A part of me wished he could.

I blinked slow and stared back at the general. "Yes, sir. Just as I'm sure your God speaks to you. Unless… he doesn't, sir." I leaned away from the microphone. "If that isn't the case, then I feel sorry for you, sir."

Lutz laughed so hard he lost concentration and fell through the table. Casey snorted and I was trying hard to keep a straight face.

"Captain, I've had just about enough of this." Marshmallow was starting to look like the real thing when you hold it just far enough out of the flames it doesn't burn, but puffs up really big.

Hardass wasn't even looking at me, or at Marshmallow. He leaned on his arm with the tattoo, his mouth buried in his palm.

My commander's face was the darkest red I'd ever seen. Having gone this far, I glared at Marshmallow. "So have I, sir. If you continue to disparage my religion, I will be forced to file a complaint to the Pentagon, sir."

"Stop, stop, please…" Lutz was trying to get off the floor. "You're killing me!"

Casey snorted even louder. "You're already dead." He tried to whisper, but not too effectively in the small room."

"If you're referring to the Captain's career, Mr. Delgado, you're right!"

Gen. Hardass dropped his hand and turned to face Marshmallow. "That's Commander Delgado." He said it even slower than I had spoken. "He is the Southwestern Regional Commander of Border Patrol. Address him with the respect due one of our other branch officers."

The glaring match shifted from me to the two generals. Marshmallow caved first. "I apologize, Commander Delgado. Returning to the matter at hand. This hearing has gotten out of hand and the sarcasm will be noted in your file, Captain Castle."

Casey stood up and leaned over my shoulder to the microphone. No smirk on his face. "That's Captain Delgado, sir. You disrespect my rank and her religion. Our marriage is one thing I will not allow you to contest. Captain Del…gado."

Lutz took up Casey's snorting.

I took a deep breath, focusing on Hardass. "Sir, I have nothing else to say. Do as you will. I am tired and wish to go home for a few hours, before I must preside over the spiritual release of those who died." I looked to Lutz. "Their souls have lingered here long enough."

"Captain Delgado." Hardass ignored the microphone. "We have heard enough. You are dismissed. See to your family and friends."

I slowly stood up as he did, thankful to be released, though Marshmallow looked like he wanted to go a few more rounds. Hardass didn't let him, walking around the table. My commander took a moment to snap out of his 'what the hell is going on' coma and jumped to his feet.

"Officers Delgado." He addressed us both.

"General Marquez." Casey squinted at him slightly as he extended his hand. "Is this over yet, or are you taking it to a full tribunal."

Leave it to Casey to cut to the quick. Hardass gave him the same squint back, giving a firm handshake. "Based on what we've heard and without evidence to the contrary, it would be difficult to proceed to that extreme."

"But I will be discharged, no matter what the decision, sir." I didn't hold out hope otherwise.

"That remains to be seen. It will take some deliberation. Not trying to be prejudiced, but you have to respect what it would be like if your base priest was suddenly promoted to the U.S. Cardinal position. The Marines would find it difficult to decide where he fits."

"Understood, sir."

Casey took my arm in his. "If I can take my wife home to rest, sir."

"Of course." He stepped out of my way. "Until you hear from us, you are released to medical leave. And your tribal duties. The U.S. Marines offer condolences to those your… the Earth People, lost in this unfortunate incident. I do not envy the task, as the Ci'in, you must face. Go, knowing we won't interfere in your religious services."

CHAPTER

38

As much as I wanted to go home and sleep, there was someone else who needed my attention. The Marines brought Sabrina out for Lutz' military funeral. She'd been told the official story and helped to clear his affairs, all while we were still in the hospital.

It was quick, formal and cold. With papers signed, they expected her to go away. My mother intervened and took Sabrina to the last place Lutz had slept. Our apartment. Sabrina could feel him there, smell him on the pillow. In the clothes he'd left behind. It gave her more time to accept what had happened.

I had no doubt Lutz visited her there, when he wasn't heckling my proceedings. But time was up. Chucky carried me up the stairs, since Casey couldn't. I half-expected him to slam my head into the wall, but he didn't. He put me down rather gently, backing off with no snide comment about needing to lose weight.

Casey took his place, wrapping his good arm around me. It was the first time I'd been back here. It felt weird knocking on my own door.

My mother answered, letting us in. Sabrina stood up from the sofa to greet me.

"I'm Beth, Brandon's partner."

Sabrina looked me up and down for a second. "I recognize you from the pictures Brandon sent." Her arms gently wrapped around my shoulders. "Thank you." Her voice cracked slightly. "I appreciate the time you've given me here." She let me go, taking my hand and leading me to the sofa. She didn't let go, helping as I eased myself down. "Are you sure you should be out of the hospital?"

"The infection is gone, the wounds closed. I just have to rebuild my strength." I let out a breath and leaned back as Casey added a pillow behind me and sat on the sofa arm. "I'm more concerned about you, Sabrina. I'm so sorry this happened."

She dropped her eyes. "He was a soldier. We talked about this a million times. Planned for the worst..."

"But never quite believed it would happen."

She nodded. "I should have wrapped things up and moved out here sooner." She plucked at some little piece of fuzz on her shirt, rolling it in her fingers. "It might have been that pebble in the ocean and he'd still be here."

I didn't try to suggest fate finding us, regardless. Lutz' priorities might have changed all sorts of things we did. Our schedule might have shifted. I might not have noticed the second trail. We might not have run into the zombies. Not for a while yet.

"We can't live our lives asking 'what if'. He doesn't want that. His Spirit wants you to find the peace to go on without regret."

"I know." She raised her head, looking around the apartment. "He said that to me before the last tour. No regrets. I just need time to reach that point." She reached out for my hand again. "Letting me stay here, instead of rushing me off like everyone on the base did, means a lot. Thank you."

"You can stay as long as you need to." I squeezed her hand. "But tonight…"

"The ceremony. Your mother explained your ways. Earth people and spirits. You'll call him and the others who died and do a ritual to release their souls out into the universe so they can be reborn." She smiled. "He wasn't big on religion, but I think he'd get a kick seeing if it's real."

"He will. I learned that much about him in the few months we worked together. Like you, I wish there was more time." I looked up at Casey and back to my brothers. "Can you guys leave us alone for a while?"

They nodded and Casey gave me a kiss on the forehead. My mother went into the kitchen as they left. I waited a moment and with just a silent thought Lutz appeared for me. My mother came back into the room, setting down two cups of tea. I picked up one, handing it to Sabrina.

She took it. "Thank you, but I'm not a tea person."

"It's not really tea." I gave her a raised eyebrow. "Brandon wants to speak to you before I release his Spirit. This softens the psychological barriers your culture builds up. It also might make you a bit sleepy, but won't hurt you otherwise."

Sabrina looked into the cup, then at me. I expected refusal, at the very least a few questions, but she downed the cup in four slurps. “Now what?”

“Let’s go to your room.”

She got up quickly, helping me walk her into the guest bedroom. I sat down in the chair next to the bed. “Get comfortable. Lean back and close your eyes.” She stacked pillows up and did exactly what I asked. “Visualize Brandon here. Take slow easy breaths. Visualize, and in your mind, call him to you.”

I spoke softer and softer, watching her body relax. Ninety percent of the effect was her willingness to believe in the lavender scented herbal tea, opening herself to hypnotic suggestion. It worked and Lutz saw the moment when she drifted beyond the inhibitions controlling her.

He sat down next to her. “Sabi, I’m here.”

Her mouth opened as she gasped. “Brand… Brandon?”

“Yes, baby. I’m here.” He stroked her leg.

I leaned forward, injecting a whisper. “Slowly open your eyes. Remember, this is his Spirit.”

Sabrina didn’t open her eyes. Instead she put her hand down to where he touched her. “I’m a little afraid to look. Afraid this is a dream.”

“It isn’t. Open your eyes, baby.”

The muscles around her eyes flinched. Fear and desperation battled each other, but her need to see Lutz won out. She opened her eyes and teared up immediately. “It’s really you.” She looked down to where her hand had tried to touch his, but instead saw that she was rubbing her own leg. His hand not real. “I can’t touch you?”

“No, I don’t have a body anymore.” He reached up and stroked her cheek. Sabrina tried to touch his hand again, failing. “Some would say I’m only residual energy, which I guess is what you feel. I’m only my Spirit now.”

“So, there is something after we die.” Sabrina tried to laugh.

“Apparently, though we still have to wait to see what comes next. I just know a part of me is always going to be here, with you. And I guess I have to be glad things happened the way they did, so I’d be able to say goodbye.” Lutz glanced over at me. “Thank you. For being a friend when I was alive, and now.”

“Your strong Spirit let you do this. Strong enough to wait for this moment and strong enough to let go when the time comes.”

“Do you have to, let go that is? I mean, you hear stories.” Sabrina sounded a little scared and hopeful.

“Haunting? That wouldn’t be good for his Spirit. Those who can’t find their way to the next… life, they get lost in this one. In time he would stop being the man we knew. Kind of like Alzheimer’s. Neither of you want that.”

“Nooo…” She sighed, staring into Lutz’ eyes. “I’d never want that to happen to you. I love you too much to ask you to live… to exist, like that.” She reached out again to touch him, but remembered she couldn’t. “I don’t want to say goodbye yet.” Her voice cracked as tears fought to burst free. “I want to feel your arms around me. Just one more time.”

“The effects of the tea won’t last long.” I pushed out of the chair, nodding to them both as I shuffled towards the door. “You should spend it together.”

Outside the door my mother waited, holding the cup of tea I'd ignored. "You must rest too. Drink this and get a little sleep.

"I guess I can." I took the cup and she unrolled her hand, my pain meds in her palm. "Sure. I need them." I gulped them down and let her lead me to my bedroom. As nice as the resort suite had been, my own bed felt great. My mother helped me undress and then tucked me in, like I was a kid again. It felt great, especially as the pain meds kicked in.

When I finally drifted back to the surface, Casey sat up from the chair in the corner. "You feeling all right?"

"Yeah." I took a deep breath. "I just needed a nap, I guess."

"I wish we could put this off for another day." He got up and turned the lights a bit brighter. "Laid out some clothes for you. Your mother will want you to eat something."

"Sabrina?"

"Still asleep. No one's had the heart to wake her up. We figured Lutz would let us know when she did."

I looked from my clothes on the foot of the bed to the clock. "Maybe a few more minute. Help me?"

"For the rest of our lives."

Between the two of us, I managed to get dressed. Casey was babying me as much as my family, even though he was still recovering too. I went along with it, knowing it was only a matter of time before I lost part of them forever… no, until my time came.

CHAPTER

39

I gave them an hour more, then slipped into the room, she was asleep. Lutz lay next to her, his arm draped over her. She slept with her hand clutching one of his t-shirts.

Lutz didn't look at me. "She's dreaming of…"

"You don't have to share." I whispered. "Hope she had some closure."

"We both did, but it's time for me to go." He embraced her one more time, kissing her cheek, then slipped away. "I'll join you later." He disappeared, clearly not wanting to say the final words to her. Or hear them. Probably for the best.

I went to Sabina and watched her sleep for a few more minutes. When her eye movement changed, I put my hand on her shoulder. She murmured, then blinked. "He's gone."

"Yes, until the ceremony to release his Spirit. You don't have to go if it's too much."

She sighed, pulling the t-shirt to her face. “I should, but I really don’t feel the need now. Can I go back to sleep?”

“Of course. Stay. Dream a little more.” I left her as she held Lutz’ t-shirt to her face. She was instantly back to her dreams.

In the living room everyone waited. Quietly. Next to the door were my parents’ suitcases. Joey had joined us. I went to the patio where he was talking on the phone. “Yeah, we’ll be there on time. Just have the clearances.” He hung up. “You should be with mom and dad.”

“And not get a few minutes with you?”

He tucked his phone into his pocket. “I never was good at saying goodbye. Ask my ex-girlfriends.” He tried to make it sound funny, but neither of us laughed. “Just finalizing the plan. Not an easy task in this day and age, making us all disappear.”

“Monumental, to say the least. Not at all thrilled that I have to be the one to do it.”

He leaned against the patio railing. “Most of thc elderly are opting to pass with their current tribes. What happens on the Res…”

“Stays on the Res. Yeah, but a thousand or so people all dropping dead at the same time will be noticed.”

“It’s all in the staging.” He looked away when I winced. “A hundred years ago, no one would notice. But as things got so regulated, we knew we had to have a plan. The last fifty years we’ve been putting people in the right places. With your recovery and hearing taking this long, we had extra time to finalize the arrangements.”

“Glad my inconvenience worked out for you.”

Joey laughed. "You're definitely healing, Sis. Chucky was afraid the Ci'in sucked all the spunk out of you."

I shrugged. "Then he should have been at the hearing."

"Yeah, heard you were tearing them up with the witty come-backs. Lutz said he never laughed harder."

"Tell me about it." I joined him against the railing, leaning on my good hip. My chest felt tight. "This is way harder than I thought it would be. I'm sure it's hard for everyone else too."

"It is, but deep down it's what we all want. Even you."

"Yeah, but doesn't make tonight any easier." I leaned my head onto his shoulder. "I'm going to miss you."

Joey wrapped his arm around my shoulder. "Ditto, Sis."

We stood outside for a little while, before Daniel opened the door. "It's time."

Inside everyone was waiting for us. I turned to look up at the evening sky. It was clear of clouds. The stars would be bright tonight. "Okay. Let's go."

Chucky carried me down the stairs and into the truck, sitting me in the back between my parents. Casey drove and Joey was in the passenger seat. Daniel, Frankie and Chucky followed as we drove across the city to the Yuma airport.

"Everything is ready?"

Casey rolled his window down, showing an ID and getting waved through. Joey gave the guard a nod before we drove on. "It's all arranged. We've got people all over the Nation in place to process us through the airports."

Casey turned to drive between two large hangers.

“We’ve arranged a flight to take us to a Pow-Wow outside of Miami, a leased Boeing Super 7. Unbounds have been converging at collection points for the last two weeks.”

“A Super 7?” We emerged from between the buildings and I saw the massive airplane ahead of us. “That’s huge. What’s the capacity, 5-600?”

“Big enough to resolve at least half our problem of disappearing.” Joey’s face tightened up as we followed the guide lane onto the tarmac.

It took a moment, then my stomach took a turn. “You’re going to crash it with everyone aboard? You can’t do that. You can’t kill yourselves. The pilots. The crew.”

“Hush, Din’ah!” My mother took my hand, squeezing it hard. “You know that’s not how it works.” Using my real name made me focus on who we were under the flesh.

“A Super 7 holds 800 at max capacity. We’re about half-full now. Then we head to Chicago, then down to Ft. Lauderdale. That’s the flight plan.” Joey turned around. “I’ll text you when we’re over open water.”

“The pilots and crew?”

“Unbound Ci’inkwia. Legitimate Boeing flight crew.” My father answered. “Every generation prepared for this, we just never shared it with everyone. Need to know.”

“And it will be painless.” A comforting pat of my mother’s hand accompanied her reassurance.

“Remote autopilot will carry the plane past Florida, down into the Puerto Rico Trench.”

“The military will scramble jets as soon as the plane goes off course and gets no response from the pilots.” I knew how that worked. Everyone did. The war on terrorism was unending.

"They'll see it's heading away from populated areas and will fly in for a visual. If they get one they'll see the pilots are down and assume something went wrong with pressurization, and everyone suffocated. At that point they'll have to decide whether to follow it until it runs out of fuel and crashes, or take it down themselves. Public safety and all."

"Sounds like everything is covered." I stared at the jet as Casey swung the truck around to a group of people standing at the bottom of the stairs. Waiting for us. I didn't rush to get out of the truck. Every second seemed to escalate my mortal emotion, despite knowing this had to be done. Tonight.

My parents were helping Joey with their bags, following him as they headed for the team of TSA agents. They tagged and scanned the suitcases, following all the federal protocol for any outsiders who happened to be watching.

Casey stood at the door. "I know this is hard on you, but you need to get out and say goodbye to them."

"I know." I reached for him as I slipped out of the backseat, clinging to him a moment. "Hang onto me."

He did, guiding me to the six women and two men standing by the stairs up into the Super 7. They all wore the charter's uniform of tan slacks and white shirts, with ties or scarves with the company logo, appropriately a Thunderbird. The women's dark hair was pulled back at the base of their necks.

I recognized their Spirits, as they did mine. They stared back at me as I finally pushed myself towards them. I had to be Din'ah. Not Beth.

"Sister." The oldest of them, maybe in her forties, stepped forward, holding her hands out to me. "Thank you for joining us tonight."

"It feels necessary, though in the old days it wouldn't be so complicated."

"No, but we had no idea it would take so long." The woman looked to the airport further down the tarmac. "Who would have seen this civilization finally grow so quickly? They staggered about for so long."

"And they have a long way to go yet." I looked to the other crew. "You will take our People home?"

"We will, though you will be the one to release our Spirits." The older woman smiled and gestured to the plane. "I should finish pre-flights."

"Certainly, Captain." I released her hand as my parents came up behind me. She headed for the stairs, followed by one of the men and half the crew.

"It's time." My mother embraced me, hugging me tight, kissing me. She gave Casey the same hard embrace. "You take care of her, son."

"I will. I swear." Casey wrapped his arm around my shoulders.

"I'm sure you will." My father extended his hand to Casey. "You are both on the same path now. It is a journey that should be taken slowly, so you remember each joyful step."

Casey nodded at the advice. "Definitely a journey I have been waiting for."

My father gave me a hug just as suffocating as my mother's, then let me go. He took my mother's arm and led her up the steps.

Joey took their place. "Okay, dude. Dito what they said, because if she doesn't kick your ass, they will." He jerked his thumb at my other brothers. Casey laughed. "Sis, you were always my favorite sister."

I punched his shoulder. "I'm your only sister."

"Yeah, but I meant ever. Out of all the sisters I've had in all my lives."

The 'awww' moment made my eyes tear up, which earned me a hug. "I'll miss you."

"Take it easy on Francis." Joey whispered in my ear. "You were always his favorite too, now and before. He took the obligation of taking care of you so serious because of a prior life mistake. Way back, which is why he's been so crazy since you went Marines. Now you can just be his little sister again."

"Really?" I gave Frankie a glance where he stood next to Chucky, not looking at me. "I don't remember…"

"Like you've had the time to measure each life." Joey rolled his eyes at me. "All debts are paid now."

"Well, thanks. I'll try to be nice to him." I gave Joey another hug. "Still miss you most."

"Time to go." Daniel broke us up. "Flight's on a schedule."

"Okay." Joey let go and ran up the stairs. "I'll text you."

I waved back, unable to say anything. The rest of the crew boarded and brought the door in. Casey pulled me away from the stairs as a guy jumped into the control seat to disengage the stairs and pull it away from the plane. The TSA agents headed for their vehicle to clear the runway.

As the engines were revved up to taxi the plane away from us, Daniel herded us back to the trucks. Ground crew waved the plane out onto the tarmac, waving them into the lineup for take-off. Slow, but too fast. My heart ached, pounding painfully faster with their acceleration. I thought it would explode as the wheels left the ground.

Only Casey kept me from running after them in an insane display of grief. He urged me into the backseat, Daniel taking over the driving. He waited until I couldn't see the plane anymore. "We have another task to prepare for." He didn't expect me to answer, driving off the tarmac.

No one spoke as we headed back to the resort, back to our penthouse suite. A real cup of special tea had me out in minutes, in Casey's arm. Not enough time to mourn. When I woke it was dark, way past sunset.

Stephanie and Olivia arrived to help me dress. Since I was already the Ci'in, I didn't need to be purified with a bath, but they still sent the smoke of 'herbs' wafting through the room to soothe our Spirits. Probably for the best or I'd start crying.

Dressing in the silky buckskin and my blood-feather belt, they delivered me to Casey. He took me down to the river, to the private section where I'd meditated. On that pristine beach were Bound Ci'inkwia and our mates, sitting in a semi-circle. I sat facing them.

The strongest of the other Ci'in formed a crescent around me, completing the circle. In the center of the circle were empty blankets, one for each of the fallen, woven with patterns to represent the tribe that had been their Earth home. One was a Cocopah blanket.

Our dead had been buried at the same time as Lutz, but their Spirits were here, waiting. I could feel them. Facing the east, I could see a lightening of the sky. Morning was breaking over the distant mountains, revealing stormy clouds. It was time.

We sang to our Spirits. We sang for all the fallen and one by one they appeared in their places before me. When I called upon Lutz, he popped in and dropped down on the Cocopah tribal blanket. I half-expected a quip, but he remained quiet as we sang for those who were Unbound or chose to leave now.

It was a song carried across the nation, simultaneously. Carried by phones left open to the many tribes. My phone was before me, open to Joey. They were over the ocean now, so everyone aboard heard the song.

The Ci'in with me glowed with the light of a full moon, giving me their strength as I sang louder. I sang alone, even as lightening crackled in the distance. Thunder fittingly rolled like drums behind my voice. Before me the Spirits also started to glow, turning translucent. Turning into pure light.

I sang louder and stronger, my full Ci'in opening the path home for them. They burned with the full energy of their true beings, then spiraled up and away. I sang the last words as Lutz leaned his head back and shifted into his own energy.

He swirled towards me, brushing against me in a final touch. A final message that almost made me start crying. The phone in front of me went dead. The storm clouds opened up as he flew away. He was gone.

They were all gone.

ABOUT THE AUTHOR

T.L. Smith was born in Louisiana, but calls Phoenix, Arizona home, between bouts of wanderlust. Even a stint in the U.S. Air Force, as a radar specialist training pilots in enemy detection, brought her back to the desert.

Her time in the service taught her to appreciate the military culture and ever-changing technologies. Experience gives life to the Science Fictions she loves so much and helps her write about the strong women, holding their own as humanity reaches out into the universe.

Check out her current releases and where you can meet her at:

www.tlsmithbooks.com

or at her blog:

http://tlsmith-sfauthor.blogspot.com